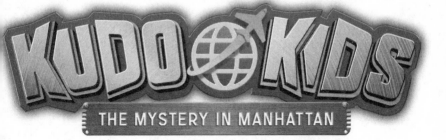

KUDO KIDS
THE MYSTERY IN MANHATTAN

MAIA AND ALEX SHIBUTANI

WITH MICHELLE SCHUSTERMAN

ILLUSTRATED BY YAOYAO MA VAN AS

RAZORBILL

RAZORBILL

An imprint of Penguin Random House LLC, New York

First published in the United States of America by Razorbill,
an imprint of Penguin Random House LLC, 2021

Text copyright © 2021 by Maia Shibutani and Alex Shibutani
Illustrations copyright © 2021 by Yaoyao Ma Van As

Razorbill & colophon are registered trademarks of Penguin Random House LLC.

Visit us online at penguinrandomhouse.com.

LIBRARY OF CONGRESS CATALOGING-IN-PUBLICATION DATA

Names: Shibutani, Maia, 1994– author. | Shibutani, Alex, 1991– author. |
Schusterman, Michelle, author. | Ma Van As, Yaoyao, illustrator.
Title: The mystery in Manhattan / Maia Shibutani and Alex Shibutani ; with
Michelle Schusterman ; illustrated by Yaoyao Ma Van As.
Description: New York : Razorbill, 2021. | Series: Kudo kids ; book 2 |
Audience: Ages 8–12. | Summary: When the Kudo siblings visit New York City,
their sightseeing plans are interrupted when a very special dress, the centerpiece
of their aunt's fashion collection, goes missing, and Alex and Mika
embark on a chase around the city to find it.
Identifiers: LCCN 2021006125 | ISBN 9780593113769 (hardcover) |
ISBN 9780593113776 (ebook)
Subjects: CYAC: New York (N.Y.)—Fiction. | Brothers and sisters—Fiction.
| Japanese Americans—Fiction. | Fashion—Fiction. | Mystery and detective stories.
Classification: LCC PZ7.1.S5167 Mt 2021 | DDC [Fic]—dc23
LC record available at https://lccn.loc.gov/2021006125

Printed in the United States of America

1 3 5 7 9 10 8 6 4 2

Design by Maria Fazio
Text set in New Baskerville ITC

To our amazing readers around the world . . .

Thank you for joining us on this adventure.

Much love,

Maia and Alex

CHAPTER ONE
MIKA

MIKA KUDO SAT CROSS-LEGGED in her chair facing the giant windows that looked out onto the tarmac at the Los Angeles International Airport. The silhouettes of planes were barely visible against the plum-purple sky.

But Mika wasn't watching the planes. Instead, her attention was fixed on her screen as she used the camera on her phone to follow the progress of a tiny, bright-red ladybug that slowly made its way up the glass.

"Why did we have to fly now? It's still the middle of the night!" Mika's brother, Andy, asked as he yawned and stretched his legs out. He offered her a paper bag, and inside she could see two muffins: one blueberry and one chocolate chip.

"Ooh, thanks," Mika said, plucking the chocolate chip muffin out of the bag. "And it's not the middle of the night. The sun is coming up soon!"

"Soon? Nuh-uh. No sun means it's still nighttime," Andy said in a deadpan voice before taking an enormous bite of his blueberry muffin. "We've been here for over an hour already!"

Karen Kudo cleared her throat as she took a seat on the other side of Andy. "Well, we left earlier than usual just in case *someone* forgot anything important at home," she said with a pointed look at Andy.

Mika stifled a giggle as Andy rolled his eyes. Last summer when the Kudos traveled to Tokyo, the family had been on their way to the airport when Andy realized he'd left his phone at home. They'd turned around to get it and ended up sprinting through the airport to make their flight.

"I think traveling feels better this way. Much less stressful." Tom Kudo took the seat on the other side of Mika, holding a tall to-go cup of coffee. "Family sitting time is more relaxing than family sprinting time. I don't want to pull a hamstring."

"Okay, okay," Andy grumbled good-naturedly. "That was almost a whole year ago! I've gotten better about waking up on time, haven't I?"

"You have," Mom agreed with a smile. "Wow, I can't believe Tokyo was almost a year ago."

"Me either," Mika said, finishing her muffin. "I was so nervous about starting sixth grade. But it's been the best year ever!"

It was true. Mika absolutely loved middle school. The classes were challenging, but her grades were very good, and she and her best friend Riley had the same lunch period, which made school extra fun. Mika loved bumping into Andy in the halls between classes—it was awesome to be at the same school as her big brother again. Plus, she was super busy with lots of extra-curricular activities. The trip to Tokyo last summer and her experience at the Summer Olympics had inspired Mika to try new things more often. She joined the cross-country team and surprised her family by auditioning for a role in the school play.

But even with all of her fun new activities, photography was still Mika's passion. She was the youngest kid in photography club, and while she'd found it intimidating to be around so many seventh and eighth graders at first, the club's meetings had quickly become Mika's favorite time of the week. Everyone had fun and supported each other, and Mika enjoyed being surrounded by other kids who loved taking photos as much as she did—it was all about creativity and expressing yourself. Every week, Mrs. Ibarra would give the club a different photography assignment, and it was so cool to see how each student came back with such different photos. "Everyone sees the world differently," Mrs. Ibarra would say to the class as Mika marveled at all of the unique perspectives.

After a big fundraiser in the fall, the school had purchased several cameras and lenses for the club. Students were allowed to borrow the cameras, sometimes even over the weekend, and Mika quickly became obsessed with learning how to use them. The photos Mika took on her phone were really good, but she thought the pictures she captured on the school's cameras were next-level. Looking through the viewfinder and adjusting the settings felt so professional.

Before the start of the school year, Karen and Tom Kudo had agreed Mika could be on Instagram as long as they were given access to monitor her account and her posting didn't distract from schoolwork. Like the loyal best friend she was, Riley still liked and commented on every picture Mika shared. So did Emma Botha, Mika and Andy's friend from Tokyo who lived in South Africa.

While Mika still loved taking photos on her phone, she couldn't help thinking that having her own fancy camera, like a real professional, would totally up her game.

Like right now, with the ladybug. Mika watched it climb higher and move farther away. If she took a photo on her phone, there was no way she would be able to capture the vivid red color and small details like she could if she had one of the cameras from school.

Mrs. Ibarra had given the photography club an assignment for spring break: curate a collection of photos that captured a theme. This assignment was special because each student could choose their own creative concept.

The only problem was, Mika had no idea what her theme was going to be.

"Good morning, passengers at gate B7. In just a few minutes, we will begin boarding flight 324 to New York City, La Guardia."

"Hooray!" Mika said, stretching her arms in the air as she stifled a huge yawn. The ladybug suddenly took off, tiny wings fluttering madly as it flitted completely out of sight.

"Good morning? The sun *still* isn't up," Andy pointed out, shaking his head before scooping the last crumbs from his muffin into his mouth.

"We've never been on a flight this early," Mika agreed, glancing at her phone. "It's a quarter to six! I get that we had to leave extra early because of Andy, but why couldn't we do a flight at nine or ten instead?"

"Well, it's a five-hour flight to New York, plus there's a three-hour time difference," Dad explained as he got to his feet. "*And* after we land, it'll take us almost an hour to get to our hotel. I'm going to be so ready for a giant slice of real New York pizza by then!"

"Mmm, I can't wait," Mika said. "Are we going to meet up with Aunt Kei and Jenny tonight?"

"I'm afraid they're busy," Mom replied. "But we'll see them tomorrow!"

Mom's sister Kei had moved to New York City a few years ago, along with her daughter, Jenny—Mika and

Andy's favorite cousin. Jenny was in the middle of her gap year between high school and college, and Mika couldn't wait to see her and hear all about what she'd been doing.

Mika picked up her backpack and followed her parents to the line that was beginning to form at the gate. No sleeping on this flight, like she had last summer—Mika was going to get all of her homework done so she wouldn't have to worry about it during her vacation.

Next to her, Andy was reading the mystery book he'd checked out from the school library right before spring break. Mika couldn't help but wish that she was allowed to check out one of the school's cameras to bring with her to New York too—but unfortunately, that wasn't allowed.

As the line started to move forward and the passengers boarded the plane, any remaining grogginess Mika felt disappeared. In a few hours, she would be in New York City! Broadway, Central Park, Times Square . . . It was the perfect place for a photographer looking for inspiration!

MK: Riley!! I'M GOING TO NYC!!!

RJ: LOL I know!! You've only mentioned it fifty times in the last few weeks!

MK: HA HA!

MK: I mean I'm on the plane! Right now!

RJ: Yasss! Send me ALL THE PICS!

RJ: Nvm, you take so many. Just the best ones!

MK: Haha okay I will! How's Phoenix so far?

RJ: SO. HOT. 😣

RJ: But it's great to see my cousins!

MK: That's so weird—I packed a coat and boots for my trip! 😄

RJ: Is it really that cold in NYC? It's March!!

MK: Guess I'll find out soon! ✈

CHAPTER TWO
ANDY

"THIS IS US! EIGHTEEN . . . D and E," Andy said, dropping his book and phone onto his seat. He stuffed his backpack under the seat in front of him, and then began helping Mika with hers. Mom and Dad settled into the row across the aisle.

"Ooh, look at all these movies!" Mika said, already scrolling through the in-flight entertainment selection on the screen in front of her. "Want to watch one with me?"

"Sure! As soon as I finish putting your bag away. Can you stop swinging your legs for a second?" Andy replied as he struggled to slide Mika's bag past her feet.

"Oops. My bad, thanks Andy." Mika giggled.

Andy straightened up, took off his jacket, and flipped his novel open to the bookmarked page. "A movie sounds good, but I want to finish this first. I read another chapter last night and I'm pretty sure I figured out who the thief is."

"Whoa, didn't you just check that book out of the

library on Thursday?" Mika asked. "You should challenge Riley to a speed-reading competition."

"I'm not *that* fast," Andy said as he buckled his seat belt. Riley Jenkins was the fastest reader they knew. She could read an entire book in less than one day.

Even so, Andy had to admit he was a much faster reader now than he had been at the start of seventh grade. He'd liked books, but games and puzzles had always been his favorite hobby. Ever since Mika and Andy's team won the opportunity to be beta testers for a virtual-reality game company, he and his friend Tyler Smith had done lots of testing. Andy's best friend Devon joined the baseball team at school, Riley started a book club, and Mika . . . well, Mika was busy with *everything*—track, the school play, and, of course, photography club.

Given how nervous she had been before the school year started, Andy was relieved his sister was enjoying her activities so much. But even though they were at the same school now, somehow, they were spending less time together.

Andy was busy too, just in different ways. All of the amazing athletes he'd watched at the Olympics had inspired him. He started playing basketball after school with a few new friends he'd made in gym class, and discovered he was a natural. Andy loved finding different ways to score and had even started watching highlights on YouTube to pick up new moves to add to his game.

He was especially excited that as editor in chief of the popular sports website Compete, Mom was going to be covering the NCAA Tournament East Regional Finals at Madison Square Garden while the Kudos were in New York. The previous week, she had surprised them by announcing that she had gotten tickets so Mika, Andy, and Dad could come watch a game while she worked. Andy had filled out his own March Madness bracket and had been following the early stages of the tournament. It was so challenging to predict the winners of each round, but that's what made it fun and exciting.

Suddenly, Andy lurched forward and grasped for his bag.

"Uh-oh, what did you forget this time?" Mika asked with a familiar look of concern.

"Umm. Hold on. I just need to check . . . Got 'em. We're good!" Andy exhaled and sank back into his seat.

He waved a bright orange case in the air with a relieved smile. For one panicked moment, Andy was worried he'd forgotten his glasses at home. He'd had them for almost two months now, but he was still getting used to carrying them around with him. Between all of the game testing and watching so many basketball highlights, Andy's screen time had skyrocketed. His grades were still really good, but right before the holidays, Andy realized he was having a hard time reading some of the things his teachers wrote on the whiteboards at school.

Andy didn't mind wearing glasses, but his parents had been concerned that all of the time he spent on his phone was affecting his vision.

"We're not saying you need to stop beta testing or watching basketball videos," Mom had said one night over dinner. "But maybe it's time to find a hobby that doesn't require as much screen time."

"Theater!" Mika said immediately, grinning at her brother. "We could use some help backstage. You can paint some of the sets or even be my personal assistant."

"Very funny," Andy replied with an eye roll. The truth was, he'd been thinking about joining a club at school ever since Mika had come home after her first day of photography club practically glowing with excitement. But none of the other clubs sounded especially interesting to him.

That night, Dad had come into Andy's room with a worn paperback book.

"*The Westing Game*," Andy read off the cover. "What's it about?"

"It's a mystery," Dad said. "One of my all-time favorites. I think you'll like it. See if you can solve the puzzle before the characters do!"

The word *puzzle* had definitely gotten Andy's attention. He'd opened the book, thinking maybe he'd read a chapter or two before bed, but he ended up staying awake way too late devouring almost half of it! The characters were awesome and the story really was like a puzzle—Andy loved trying to piece all of the clues together.

When he finished *The Westing Game*, he'd gone straight to the school library and asked Mrs. Moore, the librarian, for another mystery novel. Andy had been a regular at the library ever since. He was getting better and better at solving the mystery before the main characters.

Bzzt.

Andy glanced at his phone screen and saw a text message from Tyler.

> **TS:** I finally went to Heist House last night! Solved it in only 40 minutes. They said that's the record. Bet you can't beat that!

Grinning, Andy set his book down and typed out a response.

> **AK:** Is that a challenge? YOU'RE ON!

Then he sent a quick text to Devon, whose family was watching their dogs while they were out of town.

> **AK:** About to take off! How are Lily and Po?

> **DM:** 👍

Devon's response was accompanied by a photo of Lily sprawled out belly-up on his bed, her tongue lolling out. Next to her, Po sat up straight and stared right at the camera, his head tilted to the left. Curled up on Devon's pillow eyeing both pups suspiciously was Devon's ginger cat, Conan. Snickering, Andy showed the photo to Mika, who snorted.

"I don't think Conan likes them invading his space," she said.

"Hopefully he'll warm up to them this week," Andy replied.

He sent Devon a laughing-face emoji and turned airplane mode on just as a flight attendant passed by, checking everyone's seat belts.

"Looks like you two have a little extra room," she said with a smile. "Since no one is in the window seat, you can spread out!"

"Ooh, yay!" Mika exclaimed, unbuckling her seat belt and scooting over. "I can take photos out the window!"

Andy watched as she buckled herself in again, leaving the empty seat between them. "Mika, Tyler got out of Heist House in forty minutes!"

"Huh?" Mika's brow furrowed. "What house?"

"Heist House," Andy repeated, slightly impatient. "The new escape room I told you about . . . remember?"

Tyler had texted Andy a link to the Heist House

website weeks ago and Andy had shared it with Mika right away. The website was mysterious, but it looked like it could be the ultimate puzzle. Andy was thrilled when he'd realized that Heist House would be open by the time the Kudos visited.

Unfortunately, while Tyler lived in Manhattan, he was away in Orlando for spring break. They'd never met in person, but they had quickly become friends when Andy realized that Tyler was the only other person he knew who was as obsessed with puzzles as he was.

Tyler was very good at solving puzzles, but so was Andy. He couldn't wait to try beating Tyler's Heist House time.

"Oh, right," Mika said, pulling her headphones out of her pocket and untangling them. "That's really cool!"

"We can do it Monday!" Andy said eagerly. "I mean, I know we have a lot of stuff to do, but Dad said all of the museums are closed on Monday, and the basketball game isn't until Friday."

"Yeah, maybe!" Mika sounded distracted. "I was going to ask Mom and Dad if we could visit B&H to-morrow."

Andy frowned. "What's that?"

"It's this *huge*, famous store," Mika said, her face lighting up the way it always did when she talked about photography. "Mrs. Ibarra told me about it when I said that we were going to New York for spring break. They have cameras, televisions, and all sorts of gadgets. She said I could even try out all of the different cameras they have!"

"That sounds really cool, but we have camera stores in LA, you know."

Mika laughed. "I know! But B&H is special. Mrs. Ibarra called it a New York City institution!"

Andy smiled, even though he couldn't help feeling a little deflated. "But you want to go to Heist House too, right?"

"Yeah, maybe," Mika said again. "I'm going to start my homework once we're up in the air, but when I'm done, let's watch the first Avengers movie together."

Andy sighed. "Again? Wow, you really love that movie."

Sliding his phone into the outer pocket of his backpack, Andy tried to return his attention to his book. As their plane began to roll out of the gate and head toward the runway, Andy couldn't help but think back to all of the other trips his family had taken. Because he and Mika had shared the same interests, they had always planned out all of the cool stuff they would do together.

Now they were excited about very different things.

CHAPTER THREE
MIKA

"I STILL DON'T SEE MY BAG!"

Mika stood on tiptoe, watching anxiously as a giant black suitcase slid onto the baggage carousel and joined the others. Mom's suitcase had been the first to come out, and Dad's and Andy's bags had followed less than a minute later.

Almost ten minutes had passed and there was still no bright blue suitcase to be seen.

"Shouldn't they all be together?" Andy asked, craning his neck to look. "I mean, we all checked in at the same time."

"Yes, but the suitcases get loaded up onto a cart with hundreds of others," Dad explained. "And *then* they get put onto the plane. There's a chance that they won't always stick together. Don't worry, hon," he added when he saw Mika's anxious expression. "There are still plenty of bags coming out, see?"

He pointed, and Mika looked up hopefully. But the

bag sliding down the ramp was small and yellow.

She sighed, nervously squeezing the straps of her backpack. What if her bag never came out? Mika had packed some of her favorite cold-weather clothes to wear on the trip and she wanted to show Jenny and Aunt Kei her new jacket.

"Hey, look!" Andy said. "A blue suitcase—two of them!"

Mika brightened when she spotted the bags. "One of those might be mine!" she said. "I'll go look."

She hurried through the thinning crowd of people still waiting for their suitcases, trying to keep her eye on the two blue bags. Mika darted around a woman tying her toddler's shoe and stopped.

There was only one blue bag now. Mika pulled it off the carousel and frowned. She didn't have to unzip it and check the contents to know that this wasn't her bag.

"Where did the other one go?" she said aloud, turning around frantically. On the other side of the woman with the toddler, Mika spotted a young man wearing a gray jacket walking away—with Mika's suitcase!

"Hey!" Mika cried, dragging the other suitcase behind her. "Excuse me, sir, but I think you have my bag!"

The man turned around in surprise and peered down at her in confusion. "Huh?"

"That's *my* bag!" Mika said again, pointing to the sticker and patch on the side. "See the butterfly patch?

And that's my Tokyo Olympics sticker. I put them on here because my dad told me that lots of suitcases look alike and I wanted to make mine different."

The man looked from one suitcase to the other and grimaced. "Whoops! So sorry about that," he said, taking the other blue suitcase from Mika.

"No worries. It's all good!" Mika breathed a sigh of relief as he walked away. She dragged her suitcase back over to where her parents and Andy were waiting. "Glad I put the patch and sticker on," she told them triumphantly. "Someone else almost took my bag!"

Fifteen minutes later, Mika squeezed into the back seat with Mom and Andy as Tom Kudo and the cab driver loaded all of the Kudos' bags into the back of a bright yellow taxi.

"These are so different from the taxis in Tokyo," Andy said. "No automatic doors! And the Tokyo ones were black, not yellow."

"And they had lace seat covers," Mika remembered, buckling her seat belt. "But whoa! They didn't have TVs!"

She pointed to the small screen behind the passenger seat. The sound was low, but Mika could see a clip from a late-night talk show playing.

As the cab pulled away from the curb, Mika turned to look out the window. Why would she stare at a screen when New York City was right there?

"So, what do you guys have planned for your time in the city?" asked the cab driver, flashing a friendly smile in the rearview mirror. "I'm guessing you're all here for a little vacation, am I right? Or is this a work trip?"

"Actually, it's a little bit of both," Dad replied. "I'm a travel writer, and I'll be writing a few restaurant reviews while I'm here. And my wife is covering March Madness."

The driver's eyes widened. "Oh, no kidding? You're a sports reporter, ma'am?"

"Sort of like that," Mom said with a smile. "Are you a basketball fan?"

"You know it! Us New Yorkers love basketball . . . and baseball . . . and football . . . and hockey . . . and tennis. We love all sports! Hey, got any expert predictions?"

Andy sat up straight. "It's Duke versus USC this Friday," he said. "I have USC making it to the Final Four!"

"Is that right?" the driver said, clearly amused. "Have we got a Trojans fan here?"

"We're from LA," Mom explained. "I think my son has decided he's obligated to root for USC. As for the Final Four, right now I'm thinking USC, Michigan, Arizona, and Ore—"

"Look!" Mika cried, pressing her hand to the window. "I see Manhattan!"

"I thought we were already in Manhattan?" Andy said as he leaned over Mom to see. But the skyline had vanished behind the trees as the taxi turned the corner.

"The airport is in Queens," Mom explained. "That's a borough—a neighborhood—that's part of New York City, like Manhattan."

"It was so pretty," Mika said with a sigh. "I wish I'd gotten a picture."

The cab driver chuckled. "Don't worry—you'll get a much better view of Manhattan comin' up. Just wait till we cross the bridge!"

Mika pulled her phone out and opened the camera app. "I'm ready! Will I be able to see the Empire State Building?"

"You bet, kid!"

"It'd be so cool to see the city from above. There's an observation deck there, right?" Andy asked.

"There is!" said Dad. "That's on our list. You've got Times Square, Central Park—and of course, *all* of the eats. The diversity of food options in New York City is incredible—you can try cuisines from pretty much any culture! Matzo ball soup, giant slices of pizza you can fold in half . . ."

"Dim sum in Chinatown," Mom added. "Halal carts . . ."

"And Little Italy!" Andy chimed in.

"Don't forget the bagels," the cab driver added. "A bagel with a cream cheese schmear? Classic New York!"

"What about shawarma?" Mika asked. "Can we get that, too?"

Dad glanced at her. "How do you know what shawarma is?"

"That's what the Avengers eat after they save Manhattan!" Mika said, and her parents laughed.

"It's amazing how many movies are set in New York," Mom said.

"Hey, we should add some movie spots to our list!" Andy suggested. "Like *Night at the Museum.*"

Mom smiled. "Oh, the American Museum of Natural History is *amazing.*"

"I bet a lot of the places on our list are also movie spots!" Dad added. "Like the New York Public Library— that's in *Ghostbusters!*"

"The Empire State Building is in a lot of movies, too," Mom said thoughtfully. "*Independence Day, Sleepless in Seattle . . .*"

"Buddy visits Rockefeller Center in *Elf*—we watch that one every year!" Andy said. "And Spider-Man swings from . . . well, he swings from pretty much *all* of the buildings!"

"All *those* buildings!" Mika sat up, her heart beating faster. "Look!"

As their cab began to cross the bridge, Manhattan spread out before them in both directions. Mika took picture after picture, but she could only capture a tiny bit of the city at a time—the whole skyline would take a giant panorama! Over the water to her right, the waning sun cast a warm glow that reflected off the tops of the seemingly endless sea of skyscrapers.

Her family continued to talk as their cab navigated the streets of Manhattan, but Mika was too distracted by the bustling streets and beautiful buildings to pay attention to what they were saying. She'd been worried about finding a theme for her photography assignment—but maybe she should've been worried about finding too many themes!

Twenty minutes later, they reached Herald Square. The streets were crowded with cars and pedestrians. It seemed like everywhere she looked, Mika spotted another amazing photo opportunity. As she climbed out of the cab, she noticed a familiar building across the street.

"Macy's!" she said, pointing. "Isn't this where the Thanksgiving Day Parade ends?"

"It sure is!" Dad said as he helped pull their bags out of the trunk. After thanking the cab driver, the Kudos headed into their hotel.

"I'm going to text Kei to let her know we made it," Mom said, taking out her phone while Dad walked up to the front desk. "You guys getting hungry yet?"

"Yeah, I'm ready for pizza!" Andy said immediately, and Mika nodded.

Dad returned with key cards to their adjoining rooms, and the family headed up in the elevator. When they got to the rooms, Mika went straight to the window and gasped.

"Is that . . . it *is*!" she said excitedly. "The Empire State Building is *right there*!"

She pulled out her phone and took almost a dozen photos, then swiped through them. "Not the best," Mika murmured, wrinkling her nose. "And the lighting's not great. If I had one of the school's cameras . . ."

Mom placed a hand on her shoulder. "Didn't you use your phone's camera when you took the photo that got featured in the Enspire campaign?"

"Yeah," Mika admitted sheepishly.

"See, it's not really about the gear or the equipment," Mom said with a smile. "It's about the photographer's point of view. You're going to get some *great* pictures again this week, Mika."

Mika brightened. "Thanks, Mom."

Mom's phone buzzed, and as she read, a huge smile spread across her face. "Change of plans!" she announced, and Dad and Andy turned to face her. "Kei's schedule just opened up and she and Jenny are free for dinner!"

"Yay!" Mika cheered as Andy grinned. "So they're coming with us to get pizza?"

"Actually, Kei suggested a place close by in Koreatown." Mom glanced at Dad. "Does that sound okay?"

"Are you kidding?" Dad rubbed his hands together gleefully. "I'd never say no to Korean barbecue!"

"Same here!" Andy said.

Mom smiled as she sent a response to Aunt Kei. A moment later, her phone buzzed again. "Ooh, interesting . . . Kei says she has some big news to share when we get there!"

"How mysterious," Dad said, laughing as he zipped up his jacket.

"I wonder what it is." Mom slipped her phone back into her pocket and grabbed her purse.

"Let's go find out!" Mika was already halfway to the door and impatient for their New York City adventure to begin!

CHAPTER FOUR
ANDY

THE MOMENT THE KUDOS stepped inside the restaurant, the delicious aroma of Korean barbecue caused Andy's mouth to water and his stomach to rumble. The hostess was talking to a couple in front of them, so the Kudos hung back and waited. K-pop music blasted on the speakers and flat-screen TVs hung on the walls, all playing different music videos. In between the televisions were blown-up photos of various dishes, all labeled in Hangul. Andy and Mika had a favorite Korean restaurant back in LA, and one of the waiters had taught them to read a little bit of the Korean alphabet. He scanned the words, trying to spot any familiar dishes . . . then did a double take.

"There they are!" he exclaimed, pointing to the dining area.

The hostess waved them past, and Mom led the way to the round table where Aunt Kei and Jenny were having an animated conversation over cups of steaming tea. Andy marveled at how much they looked alike. It wasn't just their physical features; they were both *so* stylish. Wearing fitted black pants and a floral bomber jacket, Aunt Kei had her hair cut in a chic, layered pixie. The last time Andy had seen Jenny had been on a family trip to Boston, and she'd worn shorts and T-shirts like all of the other kids. But now, Jenny's dark brown hair was chopped in an asymmetrical bob, and she wore a vintage tour T-shirt with jeans and a variety of cool rings and jewelry.

"Jenny looks like a grown-up!" Mika whispered to Andy.

"Well . . . she is, kinda," Andy reminded her. "She graduated high school last year, remember?"

Jenny spotted them first and her face broke into a huge grin as she stood.

"Hey, kiddos!" she cried, pulling them both into a hug. "Oh my gosh, you've both gotten *so much bigger*! Andy, you're almost as tall as me!"

"Am I?" Andy said, turning around so they could stand back to back.

"Your hair looks really cute like that, Jenny!" Mika exclaimed. "It used to be so long!"

Aunt Kei hugged Mom first, then Dad, before sweeping Andy and Mika into her arms at the same time. "Oh, I've missed you two *so much*!" she exclaimed. Over her shoulder, Andy could see people at the other tables looking over and smiling at all of the commotion they were making. Or rather, that Aunt Kei and Jenny were making.

As everyone settled down to take their seats, Andy heard his aunt compliment Mika on her jacket. Of course Aunt Kei had noticed.

"I hope you don't mind, but we've already ordered," Aunt Kei said, looking around at everyone. "You all like Korean barbecue, right?"

"Yeah, it's one of my favorites!" Andy said eagerly. "What did you order?"

"*Galbi*, *bulgogi*, and *samgyeopsal*—that's pork belly." Aunt Kei lifted a pitcher of water as she spoke, filling Karen's and Tom's cups. "I also picked out a bunch of side dishes. We can always order more if that's not enough! Would you like some water, Andy?"

"Yes, please." Andy raised his cup with both hands and watched as Aunt Kei filled it before moving on to Mika.

"So, how was the flight?" Aunt Kei asked, setting the pitcher down. The waitress arrived with the *banchan*— small plates of kimchi, sprouts, pickled cucumbers, potato salad, and other side dishes, which she began arranging around the grill at the center of the table.

"Forget the flight!" Jenny said with a laugh. "I want to hear about *you guys*! How's life? How's middle school, Mika?"

"I love it!" Mika told her, leaning forward. "I joined the photography club!" As the waitress reappeared to turn on the grill and place the beef ribs, thinly sliced sirloin, and pork belly on it, Mika told their aunt and cousin all about the different projects she'd worked on and everything she'd learned about cameras. Andy focused on adding food to his plate as his sister talked.

"That's *incredible*, Mika," Jenny said, plucking a few sizzling slices of bulgogi off the grill with her chopsticks. She wrapped them in a lettuce leaf with some *ssamjang*, then added a few sprouts. "I'm still not over seeing your photo in that Enspire ad during the Olympics. Mika Kudo, famous photographer! Hey, when you need a professional stylist, you know who to ask!"

Mika blushed and giggled as Jenny gestured to Aunt Kei.

"How's work going?" Mom asked her sister while helping herself to some kimchi. "Any new star clients we may have heard of?"

"As a matter of fact . . ." Aunt Kei paused, smiling mysteriously. "I *did* start styling a new client—well, technically *two* new clients. A brother-sister duo called the Leons."

Andy's chopsticks slipped from his hand and clattered onto the table. "You're working with those illusionists?" he asked, just as Dad said, "Who?"

"So, Andy, you *have* heard of them," Aunt Kei said,

smiling at him as he retrieved his chopsticks. "I kind of thought you might know of them. They're pretty popular with the younger crowd. No offense," she added to Dad. Mika burst into laughter.

"I've seen them on YouTube." Andy turned to Mika. "You have, too! That video I showed you of the guy who turned a feather boa into a snake *while* the girl was wearing it? And then somehow she made it disappear inside a glass?"

Mika squealed at the memory. "*Oh yeah!* I remember that! Wow, they're really your clients, Aunt Kei?"

"Have you discovered how they do their tricks?" Andy asked.

Aunt Kei chuckled. "Oh, absolutely not! Magicians are notoriously secretive about their methods. But you know, they're performing this week—if you want to watch their act in person, I might be able to snag a few tickets for you guys!"

"That would be so cool!" Andy exclaimed, and Mika nodded emphatically, her mouth too full of rice to respond. He finished off his last bite and piled his plate with more food, listening as Aunt Kei talked about some of her other clients: a Broadway actress named Samantha Foster, a talk show host named Kim Carlson, and a pop singer named Alisa who was performing at Lincoln Center that week.

"But actually, I've got something even more exciting

going on," Aunt Kei said, her eyes sparkling. "I have an important presentation next weekend with several potential buyers . . . I'm going to unveil my *own* original line of clothing."

Mom's mouth fell open. "Kei! That's amazing—why didn't you mention this before?"

"She's been working so hard, she probably forgot to tell you," Jenny said, shaking her head. "You should see her collection, though—the theme is sustainable style."

"Can we see some of the outfits?" Mika asked.

Aunt Kei smiled. "Absolutely. There's one in particular that I can't wait for you to see. Jenny hasn't even seen this one yet. There's a secret to the design. You might even call it an *illusion*," she said with a wink.

"Sounds really special, Kei! What about you, Jenny?" Mom asked. "How's your gap year been going?"

"Honestly, it's been fantastic," Jenny replied. "I love it here in New York—it's such an inspiring place, full of energy, and it's been nice to de-stress after senior year. I've had so much fun helping Mom out with her business. I've met some really creative people!"

"Any idea about what you want to do next?" Dad asked as he put some noodles onto his plate.

"Actually . . ." Jenny took a deep breath and straightened her shoulders. "Yeah. I want to get into writing."

"Really?" Mika asked. "What type of writing? Like Mom and Dad?"

"I think I want to write screenplays. You know, scripts for TV shows and movies," Jenny said excitedly as she looked around the table.

"We love movies! You can write the next Avengers! That's Mika's favorite," Andy told her, just as Mika said, "I was in our school play this year! Acting is *so* fun!"

"Wow!" Jenny eyed her cousins. "It's cool that you guys have all these new interests! I guess we'll have lots to talk about this week while I'm playing tour guide."

Andy blinked. "Tour guide?"

"We asked Jenny to hang out with you two while Dad and I are working this week," Mom explained. "Not that you didn't do a great job on your own in Tokyo, but Jenny knows the city really well. This way you can explore even more!"

Across the table, Aunt Kei's phone lit up with a text, and she picked it up.

"This is going to be awesome!" Mika beamed at Jenny. "You can take me to B&H! Have you ever been? It's this huge electronics store that I really want to visit!"

"Sounds fun! I think my Mom's been there before. Right, Mom?" Jenny glanced at Aunt Kei and frowned. "Everything okay?"

"Ah, hold on . . . Yeah, I think so." Aunt Kei said, sounding distracted.

"No phones during dinner, Aunt Kei," Andy joked. "That's our family rule."

Dad laughed. "That's the family rule for you kids," he said pointedly. "Besides, I highly doubt Aunt Kei spends as much time staring at screens as you do."

Aunt Kei got to her feet with an apologetic smile. "Would you all mind if I step out for a moment? I need to make a quick work call."

"Of course! Go ahead!" Mom said. "So, Jenny, on Monday morning, Tom has an interview, and I've got a meeting. Think you can meet the kids at our hotel after breakfast?"

"Totally!" Jenny said. "Aside from checking out that store, what else do you guys wanna do?"

"Definitely Heist House!" Andy exclaimed. "But I'm not sure how early they open."

"Isn't that the new escape room?" Jenny asked. "I've actually never done one of those before. Is it hard?"

"Probably, but our friend Tyler says it's awesome," Andy told her. "He isn't here, but I want to see if we can beat his time."

"Well, then, obviously we *have* to do it," Jenny said. "I can't imagine anyone beating you two at solving a puzzle. The Kudo Kids are a great team . . ." She trailed off as Aunt Kei returned to the table. Phone still in hand, she sat down, her mouth set in a grim line.

"Mom, what was that about?" Jenny asked.

"Oh, it's Carrie—my assistant," Aunt Kei explained with a sigh. "She called to tell me that she has a family emergency and needs to leave the city for a few days. Nothing too serious, and of course, I completely understand. But . . . well, with this presentation on Saturday, it's not exactly the best timing."

"Oh no," Jenny said. "Can Sammy help, or maybe Tamara?"

"I just called them, but they're not available." Aunt Kei drummed her fingers on the table. "I've got so much going on with my clients this week, with all the fittings and appearances . . . I'm just not sure how I'm going to manage everything *and* prepare for this presentation."

Andy glanced at his sister, and instantly knew that they were thinking the same thing.

"We can help!" they said in near-perfect unison, and Aunt Kei looked up in surprise.

"Oh, that's so sweet of you guys," she said with a smile. "But this is your vacation! You don't want to spend it running all over the city."

"But we don't mind!" Andy insisted.

Aunt Kei looked amused. "Still, I don't think—"

"We can do it together," Jenny spoke up. "Andy, Mika, and I were going to be hanging out all week anyway. We can help you out while we're seeing the city. Right, guys?"

"Yeah!" Mika exclaimed.

"Is that okay?" Andy asked, looking from Mom to Dad.

Mom paused. "As long as you're with Jenny and you stay in touch, I don't see why not. It's sweet of you three to offer to help Kei out like this."

Andy turned to his aunt. "Three assistants are better than one, right?" he said, and Jenny nodded in agreement.

Aunt Kei's lips curled into a small smile, but she still looked doubtful. "Well . . ."

Mika drew a deep breath, and Andy knew what was coming. Snickering, he covered his ears with his hands just as Mika delivered her signature:

"PLEEEE-EEEE-EEEEE-EEEEZZZ!"

Jenny burst out laughing. "What in the world was *that*?"

"Mika's famous pitiful sheep-bleating thing she does," Dad said, shaking his head. "Hard to say no to that. Right, Kei?"

Aunt Kei's eyes watered as she tried to suppress laughter. "Absolutely impossible. But please stop. People are staring. I'd be thrilled to have you as my assistants for the week. Thank you *so* much."

Mika cheered, and Andy grinned as he helped himself to an onion off the grill. This trip was already off to an exciting start.

TS: So are you doing Heist House tomorrow??

TS: Oh wait, it's not open on Sunday . . .

TS: Monday???

AK: Maybe! We have to help our aunt with some work stuff on Monday.

TS: ☹

AK: It's fine! Our cousin is taking us to Central Park. But maybe we can do HH after that!

AK: SO I CAN DEFEAT YOU!

TS: Not gonna happen!

TS: Actually, maybe it will. You've got a better team than me. My friend Kyle wasn't really into it—I had to solve the whole thing pretty much by myself.

TS: Mika's really good at this stuff, too.

AK: Yup, she is.

AK: Enjoy your record while you've got it. You're definitely going down!

TS: We'll see! 😄

CHAPTER FIVE
MIKA

WHEN MIKA STEPPED OUT of the hotel Sunday morning, a frosty breeze sent her scurrying back inside with goose bumps running up and down her arms.

"It's *freezing* out there!" she cried. Her parents, who were sitting in the lobby and finishing their coffee from breakfast, both chuckled.

"Now aren't you glad I made you pack your coat?" Dad asked teasingly. "You wanted to leave it at home!"

"Because it's *spring* break!" Mika said, rubbing her arms. "And it was warm yesterday!"

"A cold front came in overnight," Mom explained. "There might even be snow later! Welcome to the East Coast!"

"Wow, really?" Mika imagined a blanket of snow covering New York City, and once again, she couldn't help but wish that she had one of the school's cameras to capture it. "Is it too cold to go to Rockefeller Center today?"

"Are you kidding?" Dad said with a grin. "It's the perfect weather to go ice skating!"

Mika brightened. "Oh, I forgot about the ice skating rink! Be right back!"

She hurried to the elevator and headed back to their room. Andy was sitting on the edge of his bed tying his shoes when Mika burst in, went straight for the closet, and began pulling out her coat, scarf, and gloves.

"What are you doing?" Andy asked, confused.

"It's freezing out there," Mika informed him. "Mom said it might even snow!"

"But it was warm yesterday!"

Mika giggled. "Welcome to the East Coast!"

Ten minutes later, the Kudos stepped outside. Mika braced herself, but the sun blazed bright overhead in a crystal-clear blue sky, and a shiver of excitement ran up her spine instead. As they proceeded down the sidewalk, they passed clusters of pigeons, boutiques with fancy window displays, restaurants with extensive menus posted outside the doors, and convenience stores that seemed to sell everything imaginable—toys, T-shirts, phone chargers, magazines, magnets, and mugs. When Mika tilted her head back to gaze up, she spotted what looked like giant wooden barrels perched on top of many of the buildings.

"What are those?" she asked, pointing.

"Water towers," Mom said as she pulled her scarf

tighter around her neck. "They supply water to those buildings. They're over a century old!"

"Wow." Mika let her gaze wander down the brick building across the street. Manhattan looked and felt historic, but also modern at the same time. Maybe that could be a good theme for her photography club assignment?

Stopping at a bustling intersection, Mika could see an entrance to the subway station right across the street. When the pedestrian light signaled for them to walk, Dad put a hand on Mika's shoulder.

"Always double-check for bikes, just in case," he said, pointing to the narrow bike line. "There are lots of cyclists in Manhattan!"

They crossed the street and headed down into the subway station, where they purchased MetroCards from a machine before hurrying through the turnstile to catch the next train.

"How do we know if this is the right one?" Mika asked breathlessly as the subway car squealed to a stop next to the platform.

"All of the cars on this line go to Rockefeller Center," Dad said. "Here, I'll show you on the map."

Once they were on the train, Mom and Andy sat down while Dad and Mika stood in front of the map next to the door. They clung to the pole as the subway car lurched forward.

"See? We're on this orange line," Dad said, tracing the line with his finger. "Rockefeller Center is here, and if we kept going, we'd be at—"

"Central Park!" Mika exclaimed, gazing at the long green rectangle in the center of the map. "Wow, I didn't realize it was *so* big."

Two stops later, the Kudos headed aboveground. On the escalator, Mom pulled a travel-size bottle of hand sanitizer from her purse and squirted a few drops into all of their hands.

They stepped outside, and Mika's jaw dropped as she gazed up . . . and up . . . and up at 30 Rockefeller Plaza. She fumbled for her phone, holding it high and doing her best to capture as much of the building as possible.

The Rink at Rockefeller Center was surrounded by the flags of different countries and was below street level, allowing people to watch the skaters from above. While Mom rented skates, Mika took as many pictures as she could of the rink, zooming in on the bronze statue of Prometheus as skaters whizzed by. The environment with all the colors reminded her of the Olympics.

"I can't believe we're ice skating outside on spring break," Mika said as she laced up her skates. "This is so funny! It feels like Christmas!"

"This isn't exactly an LA spring break activity," Mom agreed.

Mika brought her phone out onto the ice—she just

had to get photos of Rockefeller Center from the middle of the rink! And while most people on the ice seemed to be skating for fun, a few of them were practicing turns and spins with confidence and grace.

"Want to race?" Andy asked, nudging her with his elbow. "First one to finish a lap wins!"

"Maybe in a few minutes." Mika turned as a particularly elegant skater zoomed past. "I just want to get a few more shots."

It took more than a few minutes to get shots she was happy with. Once she was done, Mika joined Andy in laps around the rink. Neither of them had been skating for over a year and they had forgotten how slippery the ice could be. After some flailing and a few funny tumbles, Mika and Andy found their balance and even felt comfortable enough to try skating backward. It was such a magical feeling to be on the ice in the middle of New York City!

When their feet felt cold and achy after over an hour of skating, Mika and Andy followed their parents off the ice. While Dad returned their skates, Mika, Andy, and Mom went to warm up and got four cups of hot chocolate.

"Mmm." Mika closed her eyes, savoring the steaming, sweet drink. "It's almost like pudding, it's so creamy!"

"This is *for sure* the best hot chocolate I've ever had," Andy agreed, wiping away a chocolate mustache. Too late. Mika had already snapped a photo.

"What's next on our list?" Mom asked. "Want to check out the NBC gift shop? I saw *The Office* mugs in the window, and I think that's going to be my souvenir for the week! Maybe a *Saturday Night Live* T-shirt, too."

"We should get I LOVE NY T-shirts," Andy added.

"What about Times Square?" Mika asked Dad. "Can we go there today?"

"Actually, Mom and I were hoping to do that on Thursday morning with you guys since we're both free," Dad said. "Times Square is especially crowded on the weekends, and we thought a weekday morning might be a little better."

"We can visit Grand Central Terminal on Thursday, too," Mom added. "It's very close to Times Square."

"Do you think Aunt Kei and Jenny will want to come?" Andy asked.

Dad chuckled. "No . . . To be honest, I think most people who live in the city tend to avoid Times Square. It's very touristy."

"Besides, Kei's going to be busy preparing for her presentation on Saturday," Mom pointed out. Smiling a little wistfully, she said, "Kei works so hard . . . Fashion is a tough industry, and I know she's been dreaming about this for a long time."

"Starting her own clothing line is a big risk," Dad added. "But I'm sure it's going to be a huge success. It was good of you two to offer to help her out this week," he said, giving Mika a one-armed hug. "Hopefully you'll still be able to see most of the places on your list!"

"I'm sure we will," Mika said. "Jenny said she'd take us to Central Park tomorrow. We're going to check out the zoo there!"

"Perfect!" Mom replied. "It's supposed to be a little warmer tomorrow, too."

"It's chilly, but it's such a clear day . . ." Dad mused, staring up at the sky. "Maybe we should do the Empire State Building next. It's not far from here."

Mika's mouth was too full of delicious hot chocolate to answer, but she nodded so hard that her hat slipped, covering her eyes. She shifted it back onto her head, but too late. Andy had already snapped a photo. "Ha! Gotcha back!" he teased.

Half an hour later, Mika wished more than ever that she had one of the school's cameras. Out on the Empire State Building's observation deck, she scanned the sprawling city below her. Central Park was so much bigger than she'd imagined, an expansive stretch of green bordered on all sides by skyscrapers glinting white and gray. Two rivers, the East and the Hudson, could also be seen from their vantage point.

Mika and Andy slowly walked around the entire deck until they were facing south. The buildings were even taller here, and the Freedom Tower, in particular, stood

out among the rest. Everything seemed to sparkle under the sun, the buildings, the water, the ferries . . . Mika took photo after photo, trying to capture it all.

"Hey, we're so high that the city kind of looks like LEGOs from up here!" said Andy, gazing out at the streets below. "Remember the LEGO sets we built when we were little? We would take up the entire kitchen table!"

"Mm-hmm. Sure." Mika zoomed in on the Freedom Tower and snapped another shot. When she finally turned away from the view, she realized that Andy had moved on to another part of the observation deck without her. Mika frowned slightly.

Why had he left her? Was her brother annoyed with her? Mika watched him for a moment, trying to think of what she might have said or done to irritate him. Then she shook her head. He was probably just trying to take in all of the sights.

Maybe it was all just her imagination, but she hurried to catch up with him.

Monday morning, Mom and Dad left extra early for their meetings, but not before going over the rules one more time.

"Don't wear headphones, so you can hear oncoming traffic," Mom said.

"Look both ways before you cross the street," Dad added. "And remember to keep an eye out for—"

"Cyclists!" Mika and Andy chorused in unison, and Dad grinned.

"Good to know you guys listen sometimes!"

Mika and Andy ate breakfast in the hotel's lounge area, then moved to the lobby where they had agreed to meet Jenny. Mika scrolled through her photos on her phone while they waited. She had already taken hundreds of pictures . . . and she still didn't have a theme.

"Can't it just be 'spring break in New York City'?" Andy asked.

Mika bit her lip. "That's not really what Mrs. Ibarra is looking for. She said that a collection of photos should tell a story."

"'Spring break in New York City' is a story! And how are you supposed to tell a story without words?'"

"It's . . . more specific." Mika flailed her hand, trying to search for the best answer. But the truth was, she didn't exactly know how to explain it. When Mrs. Ibarra showed them the collections taken by professional photographers, Mika totally understood how pictures could tell a story. But doing it herself was another matter entirely.

"There's Jenny—and Aunt Kei is here, too!" Andy said, leaping to his feet and waving. Mika stood, tucking her phone in her pocket, and followed Andy across the lobby. Jenny wore a faded denim jacket over a tie-dye hoodie with black skinny jeans, her hair just barely sticking out from beneath her baseball cap.

Aunt Kei wore a black jumpsuit with an olive-green utility jacket and a long silver necklace. "There you are!" she cried, pulling Andy and Mika into a big hug as if she hadn't just seen them the other night. "I just wanted to stop by and say hi before heading off to work."

"Are you working on your presentation today?" Mika asked.

Aunt Kei's face glowed. "You bet! I have so much to do—I really appreciate the three of you helping me out." She gestured to Jenny, who Mika noticed was carrying a black garment bag.

"Ooh, is that one of the outfits in your collection?" Mika asked eagerly. "Can we see—"

"It sure is!" Jenny interrupted. "We're taking it in to get altered, if that's okay with you guys." She smiled at Mika, but Mika couldn't help noticing that Jenny's smile didn't quite reach her eyes.

"Yeah, of course," Andy replied. "Just this one?"

"Yes! I already dropped off all of my other designs so they could be altered," Aunt Kei explained. "But this one . . ." She touched the garment bag fondly. "This is the centerpiece of my *entire* collection. I was making adjustments to it all weekend. But the tailor promised he could have it finished Thursday morning, so it'll still be ready in plenty of time!"

"So, this is the dress with the secret design?" Mika was even more intrigued now. She really wanted to see the dress, but something about Jenny's expression told her not to ask again.

"It sure is!" Aunt Kei beamed. "Anyway, I'd better run. I hope you three have a fantastic day in the Big Apple!" She gave each of them a kiss on the cheek, then hurried out of the lobby.

Mika peered up at Jenny's troubled face. "Is something wrong?" she asked tentatively.

"Ugh, you guys, I messed up big time." Jenny swallowed hard. "So, this morning when I was packing this up, the dress got caught in the garment bag's zipper, and it—well, it *ripped*!"

"Oh no!" Mika said. "But it was just an accident. What did Aunt Kei say?"

"She doesn't know!" Jenny shook her head. "You heard her—this is *the* dress. It's the *centerpiece* of her collection. She trusted me to run a few simple errands, and I totally blew it. She's going to be so disappointed."

Mika remembered what Mom had said about Aunt Kei yesterday. *Fashion is a tough industry, and I know she's been dreaming about this for a long time.* She felt a twinge of anxiety. What if Jenny's mistake ruined her presentation and cost Aunt Kei her dream?

"Maybe someone can fix it?" Andy suggested. "What about the tailor?"

"Maybe, but he'd probably tell my mom about the rip, and I don't want her to know what I did," Jenny said, biting her lip. After a few moments, her tense expression faded. "Oh, wait—Noah might be able to help! He's one of my friends and he's studying design at the Fashion Institute of Technology. I can try texting him!" She paused, looking from Andy to Mika. "Oh, I'm sorry . . . You probably don't want to spend our first day together in the city trying to get a dress fixed."

"No, let's do it!" Mika said. "I'd love to see the Fashion . . . School of . . . wha-what was it called again?"

"Fashion Institute of Technology," Jenny repeated. "Or just FIT. Thanks, you two—you're the best!"

The sky was overcast today, and the air still had the crisp bite of winter. But after a few blocks of walking, Mika started to warm up. She caught the delicious aroma of pastries as they passed a bakery, and suddenly breakfast seemed like ages ago.

The Fashion Institute of Technology was a gray building that stretched out for almost an entire block. Mika and Andy practically had to run to keep up with Jenny's fast pace as she entered the main lobby, the heels of her boots clacking loudly on the polished marble floors.

"Hey, Jenny!" someone called, and the three of them turned to see a young man with curly black hair and steel-rimmed glasses jogging toward them.

"Hey, Noah!" Jenny said. "I was just about to call

you. Thanks for coming down to meet us."

"For sure! I don't have class for another hour or so." Noah looked from Andy and Mika, then back to Jenny. "Who are your buddies? You never told me you had siblings!"

Jenny laughed. "These are my cousins, Mika and Andy. They're in town for spring break!"

"Nice to meet you," Mika and Andy said together.

"Whoa, you said that at the same time! Are you twins?"

"No!" Mika and Andy replied together, laughing. "I'm the older one," Andy said proudly.

"Got it! So, what did you do exactly?" He was eyeing the garment bag curiously, and Jenny guiltily told him what happened. When she finished, Noah reached out and unzipped the bag.

"Careful, it's right there at the waistline," Jenny told him. Mika and Andy stepped forward to watch as Noah delicately lifted the dress partway out of the bag. Mika admired the shimmery purple fabric—then cringed when she saw the tear.

Jenny let out a little moan. "It's hopeless, isn't it?"

"Not at all!" Noah said. "Look, see how it's torn along the seam? That makes it a much easier fix than if the actual fabric had a rip."

"You mean you really think you can fix it?"

"Definitely!" Noah said confidently. "Stop by sometime

after lunch to pick it up. This will be a piece of cake."

"Oh, that's amazing. You're the best!" Jenny cried, her shoulders slumping with relief. "Thank you so much!"

"Hey, I owe you one, remember?" Noah said, turning to Andy and Mika. "Your cousin is a great writer. I had a huge paper due last semester that I was really struggling with . . . but Jenny came to the rescue and helped me with some great research tips, *and* she proofread it for me!"

"You're exaggerating. It was fantastic," Jenny replied, handing him the garment bag. "You hardly needed my help."

She waved as Noah set off across the lobby. "Okay! He seemed confident he could fix it. Phew! Now we have some time to do all the touristy stuff! What do you want to do first? Central Park? The zoo?"

"Pastries," Mika said immediately. "We passed a bakery on the way here and it smelled *so* good."

Andy laughed. "We just had breakfast an hour ago!"

"But I didn't!" Jenny said. "I forgot to eat because I was so stressed this morning. Let's get some yummy pastries first."

As they headed back to the glass doors at the front of the lobby, Mika took her phone out. She walked slowly, turning in a full circle, capturing video of the bustling lobby.

"Ow!"

Something huge and heavy bumped into Mika's backside and she dropped her phone, which skidded across the floor. Stumbling forward a few steps, she turned and realized it was a cart with at least a dozen garment bags hanging from the rack.

"Oh gosh, did I hit you?" A girl about Jenny's age with pink streaks in her brown ponytail peeked around the cart at Mika. "I'm so sorry! You aren't hurt, are you?"

"I'm okay," Mika said, flustered. Another young woman, this one with dark curly hair, hurried over to pick up Mika's phone. Both girls wore matching yellow T-shirts that read ZOEY'S THRIFT SHOP across the front.

"Here you go!" she said, handing it back to Mika. "I think your screen is fine. Sorry about that! We just saw Alisa and got selfies with her, so she's still freaking out."

Mika nervously examined her phone, checking the screen and camera for damage. Once she was satisfied, she tucked the phone back into her pocket and turned to the girl with the pink streaks in her hair. "Wow, really?! Alisa? The singer?"

"Yes!" she said giddily. "I think she's visiting one of the professors. I am *so* glad we got the early shift today!"

The two girls headed off with their cart, still chatting loudly about Alisa. Mika smiled to herself as she joined Andy and Jenny outside. If only those girls knew that the famous pop star was her aunt's client!

CHAPTER SIX

ANDY

BY NOON, ANDY WAS starting to think that maybe he didn't need his heavy coat after all. It was still pretty chilly outside, but the sky had cleared, and the sun blazed down overhead. As he and Jenny left Central Park Zoo, he took his hat and gloves off and stuffed them into his pockets.

"The red pandas have always been my favorite," Jenny told him cheerfully. "The penguins are definitely a close second, though. Which animals did you like seeing?"

"The grizzlies," Andy said immediately. The six-hundred-pound bears had been sunning on the rocks when he'd walked in, but a minute later, one had slid off her rock and stood to her full height. Andy had watched in awe as the great bear gazed around sleepily before returning to all fours and lumbering off to her cave. "We got to see the giant pandas at Ueno Zoo in Tokyo. And the aye-ayes—those were Mika's favorite, right, Mika?"

Glancing over his shoulder, Andy expected to see

his sister right behind him. But Mika had stopped walking several feet back to take a photo of a man. He was sitting on a bench, crumbling up crackers and tossing them to a crowd of pigeons that had gathered in front of him.

"I don't even know what an aye-aye is!" Jenny admitted with a smile and a small shrug. "Is that some type of fish or something?"

Andy turned away from his sister with a sigh. "They're a type of lemur," he explained. "They're nocturnal and . . . Well, Mika probably remembers more about them than I do. She loved that exhibit."

"What did I love?" Mika asked as she joined them, studying the photo on her phone.

Andy shook his head. "Everyone thinks I'm the one in the family with the screen addiction," he told Jenny. "But Mika's been on her phone all day!"

He tried to keep his tone light, but a little bitterness must have seeped through. Mika looked up and frowned. "Hey, I'm not playing games or messing around! I'm taking photos for a school assignment!"

"I know, I know," Andy said hastily. "I was just kidding."

And he had been, sort of. He didn't want to hurt Mika's feelings, since he knew how seriously she took her photography. But last summer when they'd visited Ueno Zoo, they'd both been focused on the same thing: gathering clues and winning *OlympiFan* together. It had been so much fun working as a team.

Andy was starting to realize that he missed spending time with his sister. But he couldn't really say that because she was standing right there.

"Hey, Mika. Can I see some of the pictures you've taken so far?" Jenny asked.

"Yeah, sure. Here you go!" Mika handed her phone over, and Jenny swiped through her recent photos as they walked.

"*Wow*. These are legit. You are *seriously* talented," Jenny gushed. "I love this one of the little boy clapping with the sea lions! That's too funny; I didn't even notice him when we were there. Oops, hang on, I think I'm getting a call . . ."

She stopped walking and handed Mika back her phone before pulling out her own. "I missed a call from Noah—he must be finished with the dress! Oh, hang on, he's been texting me . . . Uh-oh."

Andy watched as Jenny's smile faded. A second later, her face paled.

"What is it?" he asked.

Jenny sighed heavily as she typed out a response to Noah. Then she jammed her phone into her jacket pocket and looked from Mika to Andy.

"We need to get back to FIT. Mom's dress is *missing*!"

"Ugh, I'm *so* sorry," Noah said for probably the dozenth time. He'd met Jenny, Mika, and Andy in the lobby again, and now they were all squeezing into a room with six monitors set up on a single desk. "I seriously have no idea how it happened. Oh, everyone—this is Ricky," he added as the bearded man seated in front of the monitors swiveled around in his rolling chair. He wore a gray jacket that read CAMPUS SECURITY in block letters. "Ricky, this is Jenny and her cousins, Mika and Andy."

"Pleasure to meet you," Ricky said, turning back to the monitors. "So . . . Noah, you said this dress was in workshop 205?"

"Yeah, that's right." Noah and Jenny moved closer to peer at the monitors, and Andy and Mika hung back as Ricky began to type.

"Poor Jenny," Mika whispered anxiously. "She's so worried."

Andy nodded in agreement. He felt terrible for his cousin. Accidentally ripping the most important dress in Aunt Kei's collection was one thing. But *losing* it was another matter completely!

"All right, I'm pulling up the feed," said Ricky as he strummed his fingers on the desk. "Noah, what time was this exactly?"

"Jenny dropped it off at around nine thirty," Noah replied. "I took it up to room 205, then left to grab some coffee from the break room. It's right down the hall—I was only gone for five minutes or so."

"And when you got back, the dress was just . . . gone?"

"That's right." Noah nodded as a view of the work-shop filled the screen. Andy moved closer to get a better look. The room didn't resemble any of the classrooms at their school. Instead of desks, there were three long tables, each holding four sewing machines and dozens of spools of thread. Several mannequins lined the wall to the right of the door, and the opposite wall was covered in cabinets.

The time stamp at the bottom of the screen read *09:36 a.m.* Just as it turned to *09:37 a.m.*, the door to the room opened.

"That's me," Noah said. Andy watched closely as the Noah on the screen walked in carrying a few heavy-looking rolls of fabric and the garment bag containing Aunt Kei's dress. He carefully hung the garment bag on a hook on the wall near the door. Then he heaved the fabric onto the nearest table before straightening up, wiping his brow, and walking out, closing the door behind him.

The time changed to *09:38 a.m.* Andy didn't take his eyes off the screen. He didn't even blink. Any second now, someone was going to walk into the room, and they would know who had taken Aunt Kei's dress. The air felt thick with tension, and even though Andy was anxious for his cousin, he couldn't help thinking this

was just like a scene from one of his mystery novels.

When the door to the workshop opened again, Mika let out a little squeak. A woman wearing a long, patterned skirt and a turtleneck sweater strode in, heading straight for the cabinets.

"That's Professor Miller," Ricky said.

Noah nodded, frowning. "She teaches a class in this room on Monday nights."

Andy stared at the professor as she opened one of the cabinets, removed a small bag, and closed the cabinet door. He leaned closer to the monitor as she walked briskly toward the garment bag hanging on the hook . . . and then passed it. Professor Miller left the workshop, closing the door behind her.

Noah let out a nervous laugh. "Glad my professor's not a thief," he joked. "Not that I actually thought she'd taken it. Professor Miller is really nice and very skilled. I think she's launching her own clothing line next month, actually!"

"So's my mom," Jenny told him. "The missing dress is part of her collection. It's kind of the centerpiece of the whole thing."

Noah's eyes widened. "Oh, no . . . I had no idea it was so important! Jenny, I feel awful!"

"It's okay! I know you didn't mean to lose it." Jenny smiled tightly, but Andy could tell by the way she gripped the back of Ricky's chair that she was getting more upset by the second. Andy returned his attention to the screen, watching as the time changed to *09:40 a.m.* A full minute of tense silence passed, and then it was *09:41 a.m.*

Finally, the door opened again, and everyone shifted forward.

"Wait, *what?*" Noah sounded stunned, and Andy couldn't blame him. Because it was *Noah* on the screen, carrying a paper cup. He took a sip before setting the coffee down next to the rolls of fabric on the table closest to the door. Then he walked over to the garment bag containing Aunt Kei's dress, unzipped it—and stepped back in surprise. Even on the screen, Andy could see why he was so shocked.

The garment bag was empty!

"I don't understand." Jenny looked from Noah to Ricky, as if they could explain what had happened. "No one else came in the room!"

"Huh. That is strange." Ricky tapped a few keys, rewinding the footage. Andy's pulse quickened as he once again watched Noah walk into the room and hang up the garment bag. Ricky hit fast-forward, and after a few seconds, Professor Miller walked in, took her bag from the cabinet, and walked out. Then Noah walked in again.

No one else had come in the room. And no one had touched the garment bag.

Andy let out a long, slow breath. This really was like

one of his mystery novels: the case of the vanishing dress!

As the others continued to talk, Andy pulled out his phone and opened the notes app. Whenever he was reading a new mystery, he liked to keep track of clues to see if he could solve the case before the main character. Now he had a real-life mystery to solve!

"What's Professor Miller's first name?" he asked Noah, thumbs poised and ready to type.

"Julia," Noah replied distractedly. "Hey, Ricky, can we take a look at the footage of the main entrance between nine thirty and nine forty-five?"

"Sure thing," Ricky replied.

"What are you doing?" Mika whispered, leaning over to see Andy's screen. "Professor Julia Miller . . . suspect?" She stared at Andy. "But she didn't take it!"

"We didn't *see* her take it," Andy corrected her. "Besides, she has a motive."

"She does?"

Andy nodded, still typing. "Noah said she's starting her own clothing line, remember? Just like Aunt Kei. Maybe she's, you know, trying to take out the competition or something."

Mika frowned. "We don't even know if Professor Miller knows Aunt Kei or knows about her fashion line!"

"I know," Andy said. "But we need to start somewhere. We'll just have to do some more research on Professor Miller."

"All right, here we go," Ricky said. Andy and Mika moved closer as another monitor showed FIT's lobby, just inside the front doors.

"That's us!" Mika said suddenly, pointing. On the screen, Andy watched himself and Jenny walk outside. Mika trailed behind, taking video on her phone. "Ooh, watch this. Some girls are about to bump into me with their cart . . ."

Sure enough, a moment later two girls in matching yellow T-shirts came into view pushing a cart with several garment bags on it. They bumped right into Mika, sending her phone skittering across the floor. Andy shifted his focus to scan the rest of the lobby and observe the other people coming in and out of FIT. One of the girls apologized to Mika while the other retrieved her phone, but there was still no sign of the dress. As the Mika on the screen headed outside and the two girls continued pushing the cart across the lobby, Andy spotted someone not too far behind Mika, exiting the building with a garment bag.

"Wait, hold on! What about that person?" he said, pointing.

Ricky paused the screen. The person carrying the garment bag wore a baseball cap, but all Andy could see was a bit of white hair sticking out from underneath.

"Can't quite see their face from this angle," Ricky

said. "But there's no way to know if your missing dress is in that bag."

"I think their hair is bleached." Andy pointed to the tiny piece of ponytail, then looked at the others. "See? Do you guys know any students or teachers who bleach their hair?"

"Well, there are a bunch of students who go here, but . . ." Noah snapped his fingers. "I think that could be Veronica Duncan!" he exclaimed. "I don't know her too well, but we've had a few classes together and she's always changing the color of her hair. She just got an internship at a theater . . . the Crescent! She seemed really excited about it."

"Bleached hair . . ." Jenny murmured, and Andy turned to her. She was staring hard at the screen, her face scrunched in thought.

"What are you thinking?" he asked.

Jenny frowned. "It might be a coincidence, but I saw a girl with bleached hair right outside of my Mom's office earlier this morning."

A little thrill of excitement ran through Andy. If there was one thing that he'd learned from reading so many mystery novels, it was that there was no such thing as a coincidence.

This girl with the bleached hair *might* be their next lead.

RJ: Those red pandas!!! I wanna hug one! 😍

RJ: Send more pics!

MK: I will later . . . something kinda weird is going on.

RJ: ???

MK: Long story, but the most important dress in my aunt's new fashion line just disappeared.

RJ: What? How?!

RJ: Did someone steal it??

MK: Maybe! But I mean it literally VANISHED. We watched security camera footage and everything! It was in a garment bag, and then it just . . . wasn't. 🎩

RJ: NO WAY.

RJ: That's freaky. Keep me posted!

CHAPTER SEVEN
MIKA

MIKA GLANCED AT JENNY worriedly as they hurried up the staircase leading out of the subway. Her typically carefree cousin hadn't smiled once since leaving FIT. Mika wondered, yet again, whether or not they should just call Aunt Kei and tell her what had happened.

"Keep close! The Crescent is this way," Jenny said, veering off to the right as soon as they were aboveground. Mika followed her a few steps, then stopped in her tracks as she took in their surroundings.

"Andy, it's Broadway!" she exclaimed. "Like, *Broadway* Broadway!"

Dazzling digital billboards covered the buildings on both sides of the wide street, all flashing animated advertisements for clothing brands, movies, TV shows, tourist attractions—and, of course, plays and musicals.

"*Wicked, Aladdin,*" Mika read, nearly tripping over her own feet as she hurried after Jenny. "*The Lion King . . .*"

"And look over there, Times Square!" Andy said, pointing. "I recognize it from *Captain America*!"

Mika gazed at the skyscraper a few blocks ahead. It was located in the center of the street, digital billboards covering the front of the building all the way to the very top.

"The ball!" she cried. "That's the building with the ball that drops on New Year's Eve!"

"Oh, cool. I think you're right!"

Mika pulled out her phone, wishing that they could stop walking for a few seconds. Or a few minutes. Or a whole hour. Times Square was buzzing and there was so much she wanted to capture here! But she wasn't about to ask Jenny if they could dawdle to take photos while Aunt Kei's dress was missing. There would be time to do touristy things again after they found the dress.

As they walked briskly on Broadway, Mika snapped as many shots as she could. Jenny turned onto 49th Street, and Mika saw a marquee reading THE CRESCENT.

"Oh nooo." Jenny stopped a few feet from the entrance and sighed. "Of course—it's Monday. All the theaters are closed."

"Maybe if we knock, someone will hear?" Mika suggested. Jenny moved toward the entrance, and Mika backed up to get another look at the marquee. She framed it on her phone's screen and tapped to take the photo just as Andy grabbed her elbow.

"What?" Surprised, Mika frowned at her phone. The image was all blurry.

But Andy wasn't looking at Mika's phone, or at the theater. Instead, he was staring farther down the street at the very end of the block. "I think . . ." he said slowly. Then, without finishing the thought, he broke into a jog.

"Andy! Come back! Where are you going?" Jenny called. "The theater's right here!" When Andy didn't look back, Jenny grabbed Mika's hand and hurried after him.

A bodega stood on the corner and, for a moment, Mika thought her brother was going to run inside. But instead, he stopped in front of a girl around Jenny's age carrying a tray holding four cups of coffee.

A girl with bleached blonde hair.

"Excuse me? Hi. Are you Veronica Duncan?" Andy asked as Jenny and Mika reached him.

The girl looked at the three of them questioningly.

"Um . . . yes?"

Jenny stepped closer, placing a hand on Andy's arm before he could speak again. "Hi, Veronica, I'm Jenny—I'm friends with one of your classmates at FIT. His name is Noah . . ."

"Oh." Veronica smiled, although she still looked unsure. "Yeah, I know Noah. What's up?"

"Did you happen to take a dress from FIT this morning?" Jenny asked. Mika noticed she didn't say it accusatorially at all. "It was in a black garment bag."

Veronica frowned slightly. "Yeah, I had a dress. My boss at the theater asked me to pick it up from the tailor's today. I had to wake up early this morning to get it and bring it to school with me because I needed to come straight here for work."

Mika's shoulders sagged. It didn't sound like Veronica had Aunt Kei's dress after all.

"Who's your boss?" Jenny asked. When Veronica gave her a slightly suspicious look, she added, "Sorry, I'm just wondering . . . because my mom's a stylist. She's friends with a lot of people who work on Broadway."

"Oh, cool!" Veronica's face relaxed into a smile. "His name's Jasper Nelson."

"Jasper Nelson!" Jenny exclaimed. "Yeah, my mom knows him! They went to school together. Small world! How do you like working for him?"

"It's great, but he can be pretty demanding," Veronica said with a laugh, holding up the tray of coffee cups. "Sorry, but I really need to get back in there before rehearsal starts. Nice to meet you, though!"

Mika, Andy, and Jenny watched as she hurried down the street and into the theater.

"*Demanding*," Jenny said as soon as Veronica was out of earshot. "That's a really diplomatic way to put it. Mom says Jasper is a *nightmare* to work for."

Mika noticed Andy busily taking notes on his phone. She let her gaze wander back to the theater. The marquee sparkled in the sunlight, reading THE CRESCENT, TEA FOR THREE. It was spelled out in large block letters, and directly beneath that it said, STARRING: SAMANTHA FOSTER.

"Wait, I've heard that name before," Mika said. "Samantha Foster?"

Jenny folded her arms. "Right—Mom mentioned her at dinner the other night. Samantha is one of her clients!"

Andy raised his eyebrows. "Jasper Nelson went to school with Aunt Kei, and now he's working at a show starring one of Aunt Kei's clients. Hmm . . . interesting. It's too bad we can't pursue that lead until tomorrow."

"Pursue that lead?" For the first time since they'd left FIT, Jenny laughed. "Listen to you, Investigator Kudo."

Andy's cheeks reddened slightly, but he continued. "Hey, this wouldn't be the first mystery we've solved. Right, Mika?"

Mika nodded emphatically. "We're going to figure out who took that dress," she told Jenny. "Don't worry!"

Jenny continued to look amused. "Well, with you two on the case, the thief doesn't stand a chance. Although Andy's right—there's really not much else we can do today. Noah already filed a missing-item report at school and said he'd keep a lookout." Sighing, she shook her head. "And besides, I promised to be your tour guide for the week. So let's do it! Where should we go next?"

"Anywhere! I just want to take more photos," Mika said immediately.

"Can we check out the library?" Andy asked. "We might want a break from the cold soon."

"Perfect!" said Jenny. "The library's right next to Bryant Park—maybe we can grab a snack. There are tons of great options in that area."

As they headed back to Broadway, Mika couldn't help noticing that Jenny's enthusiasm seemed a bit forced. "Are we having dinner with you tonight?" she asked as they walked.

"Yeah, I think so!" Jenny replied, sticking her hands in her pockets. "I was thinking we could get some take-out from my favorite vegetarian place. You guys haven't seen our apartment yet!"

"Oh, that'd be cool! And maybe . . ." Mika hesi-tated, glancing at her cousin. "Maybe we can tell Aunt Kei what happened. You know . . . with the dress. I don't think she'll—"

"No, no. I don't really want to do that yet." Jenny stopped walking, and Mika and Andy stopped, too. "It's not that I'm afraid of getting in trouble. I know Mom will understand that it was all an accident. But you guys, she's been working *so* hard on this project and she's really stressed about her presentation. She was depending on me and I don't want to make this week even harder for her! Especially since it's not like she can do anything to find the dress."

"But isn't she going to find out anyway?" Andy asked. "I mean, she's going to notice it's gone . . . Maybe she can just make a new one?"

"Well, right now, she thinks it's being altered with the other outfits for Saturday," Jenny said. "I'm supposed to pick them all up on Thursday. As long as we find the dress and fix it by then, she'll never know it went missing. Besides, I don't think it's something she could just whip up, if you know what I mean." She paused, looking intently from Mika to Andy. "*Please* promise me you won't tell her, okay? I wanted to help her this week—not make everything worse!"

Mika swallowed and nodded. "Okay. I promise."

"Me too," Andy said.

As they continued down Broadway, the two exchanged a glance. Even without speaking, Mika knew that Andy was thinking the same thing she was. Last summer, Mika had kept her Instagram account a secret from her parents and Andy. Just like Jenny, she had figured it would be okay as long as they didn't find out. But in the end, Mika wished she'd told her family from the start. Mom and Dad were so supportive of her photography, and if they had known about the Enspire contest, they might have given Mika permission. Instead, she had broken the rules and gotten into trouble.

But Jenny was clearly determined not to tell Aunt Kei, so Mika decided she would follow her cousin's wish and keep Jenny's secret. As long as they found the dress, everything would be okay.

Mika smiled as she breathed in the scent of fresh garlic and spices that wafted up from the warm paper bag cradled in her arms. The smell made her mouth water and it was the only thing that took her mind off her aching legs as she followed Jenny and Andy up the stairs.

"You must get a ton of exercise, living in a building with no elevator. This is a workout!" Andy joked.

Jenny glanced behind her and smiled. "You get used to it. Besides, it's only four floors! Although it does get a little tough when you're carrying a lot of stuff. You guys sure you've got all that?"

"Yup!" Mika and Andy chorused.

Each of them held a bag of food from Le Petit Plante, a cute little bistro with lots of bright green plants hanging from the ceiling. Mika couldn't wait to see Jenny and Aunt Kei's apartment. They lived on the Upper West Side, within walking distance of Central Park, not to mention lots of museums and restaurants—it all seemed so exciting!

Jenny balanced her bag of food against her hip as they reached the fourth-floor landing and pulled her keys from her pocket. Peering around her own bag, Mika looked down the hallway. The building itself was old, but in a nice way, with lots of dark wood and high ceilings.

"Here we are!" Jenny announced, stopping in front of the second door on the left. She turned the key in the lock and pushed it open, then gestured for Mika and Andy to enter first. Mika stepped inside eagerly, looking around.

"Um, I can't really see anything. Where's the light switch, Jenny?" Mika asked as she searched along the wall with her free hand.

"Oh! Here, let me get it for you—and would you mind taking off your shoes?" With a flick, Jenny hit the switch on the opposite wall and the entryway was flooded with warm light to reveal Mika and Andy standing in front of her with their shoes already off.

"You didn't have to tell us to do that! We always take our shoes off when we're at home." Andy said. "My best friend, Devon, used to wear shoes inside his house, but last year he accidentally stepped in one of Po's 'gifts' on a walk and didn't realize it until he was back in his living room. It was pretty messy."

"I remember that! Didn't his room smell like poo for a week?" Mika giggled.

"Guys!" Jenny pleaded. "Thanks for taking your shoes off, but can we *please* not talk about dog poo? We're about to eat! Let me give you the tour."

They passed a bike hanging on the wall and followed Jenny down the short hallway to the kitchen, a cozy space with bright blue cabinets, an old-fashioned-looking gas stove, and colorful decorative plates hanging on the walls. On the windowsill over the sink, Mika spotted a neat row of mason jars filled with green onions and small succulents.

"Are you growing green onions?" she asked in surprise, setting her bag on the counter.

Jenny glanced at the windowsill and nodded. "All you have to do is cut off the bulbs and keep them in water. They grow so fast, and we never have to buy them!"

While she pulled plates from one of the cabinets and selected silverware from a drawer, Andy and Mika began unpacking various boxes from their bags.

"Why'd you change your mind about getting vegetarian food?" Andy asked. "Not that I'm complaining! These chicken wings look delicious."

Jenny laughed. "I didn't change my mind! Le Petit Plante is all vegan. Those wings are made with cauliflower, and the mac and cheese is actually made with tempeh—have you ever had it?"

"No! Is it good?" Mika said, opening a box and examining the shells in creamy yellow sauce. "It looks just like regular mac and cheese to me!"

"It tastes even better, in my opinion," Jenny said. "Oh,

and you've got to try the jerk tofu and fried plantains!"

"I'm going to try *everything*," Mika informed her, already heaping sautéed kale with garlic onto her plate.

"Mika's really adventurous with food," Andy said. "Unless it's the really stinky type of cheese."

Once their plates were loaded, Mika and Andy followed Jenny into the living room. Jenny sat cross-legged in the bright red armchair near the window, while Mika and Andy sat side by side on the sofa and set their plates on the glass coffee table. In the far-right corner of the room sat an easel with a little table covered in oil paints. Bookshelves took up the wall on the left, and Mika noticed a stack of books and magazines underneath the coffee table as well. The one on top caught Mika's eye at the same time as Andy exclaimed, "That's a USC course catalog!"

Jenny's eyes sparkled as she popped a piece of cauliflower into her mouth. "Oh, is it?"

"Are you going to USC next year?" Mika asked excitedly.

"Nothing's decided yet, but I've applied to their film school," Jenny told them. "Keep your fingers crossed! I should be hearing back really soon. Maybe you two will be my LA food guides next fall."

Mika and Andy exchanged grins. "For sure! We'd love that," Mika said. She was thrilled at the idea of her cousin living in LA.

Andy took a cautious bite of mac and cheese. "Wow, this *is* really good!"

Mika nodded vigorously in agreement, her mouth already full. Her eyes moved to the window, where she could glimpse trees and vibrant green grass.

"Is that Central Park?" she asked.

Jenny glanced out the window. "No, Central Park is a few blocks in the other direction. But that's actually a park, too—it's much smaller, and it's right next to the Hudson River."

Mika opened her mouth to respond, but a soft rustling sound nearby caught her attention. She glanced at Andy to see if he'd heard it too, but he was too focused on his "chicken" wings.

"Did you get a cat?" Mika asked.

Jenny looked confused. "No, why?"

"I thought I—eek!" Mika jumped as something bumped into the side of the sofa. "What's that?"

"Oh, it's the Roomba!" Jenny exclaimed. "Sorry, I forgot to tell you to watch out for it."

Mika laughed as the flat white vacuum cleaner rolled away from the sofa and slid underneath the coffee table. "Mom bought one of those a few years ago, but we had to get rid of it," she told Jenny.

"Why? It didn't work?"

"It worked just fine," Andy said with a grin. "But Lily and Po couldn't *stand* it."

"Po couldn't be in the same room with it," Mika remembered. "And Lily just chased it and barked nonstop!"

Jenny giggled. "How are the pups doing? Who watches them when you guys are away?"

"Usually my best friend Riley watches them, but she's in Arizona this week visiting her cousins," Mika explained. "So they're staying with Andy's friend Devon."

"Does he have dogs, too?"

"No, he has a cat named Conan—like the talk show host," Andy said, snickering as he pulled out his phone. "Actually, they're getting along pretty well now. Look!"

Mika caught a glimpse of the photo of Lily and Po curled up on Devon's couch, a fluffy ginger cat snuggled between them. While Andy showed Jenny more photos, Mika polished off her mac and cheese and gazed at the bookshelf. There were a few framed photos, mostly of Aunt Kei and Jenny from over the years—but then one photo of two girls caught Mika's eye.

"That's Mom!"

Setting her plate down on the coffee table, Mika hurried over to the bookshelf and picked up the photo. She'd seen lots of pictures of Mom and Aunt Kei from their childhood, but this one was unfamiliar. They were standing side by side in front of what looked like a toy shop, judging from the window display. The sign hanging over the door was in Japanese.

"Look how much taller Aunt Kei is than Mom," Mika said with a giggle, showing Andy the frame.

"Wow, she really is," Andy agreed as he studied the photo. "They're basically the same height now."

"Maybe one day I'll be as tall as you," Mika said. "Or even taller!"

The front door opened, and a moment later Mika heard Aunt Kei exclaim, "Ooh, someone got fried plantains!"

"Hey, Mom!" Jenny called. "We picked up dinner from the bistro—there's plenty on the counter if you want some!"

"Wonderful!" Aunt Kei said, stepping into the living room and waving at Andy and Mika. "I hope there's enough left for two!"

"Why?" Mika started to ask, and then their mom's head popped up over Aunt Kei's shoulder. "Mom!"

"Hey, kids!" Mom said, beaming at them. "I finished up my interview early and met Kei at her office."

"Hi, Mom!" Andy held up the photo as Aunt Kei moved into the kitchen. "Look at this old photo of you and Aunt Kei that Mika found!"

Karen Kudo stepped forward and peered curiously at the photo. A moment later, her expression cleared. "Old?! Oh, I remember this! We took a family trip to Japan when I was eleven. It was the first time Kei and I had ever been."

"I bet that was so much fun," Mika said, remembering how excited she'd been to visit Japan for the first time last summer. But to her surprise, Mom grimaced and shook her head.

"Not really," she admitted.

Mika and Andy exchanged incredulous looks. "What do you mean?" Mika asked, right as Andy said, "But you were on vacation! In Japan!"

Mom laughed as Aunt Kei entered the living room carrying two plates. "Kei, I can't believe you framed this photo, of all things! Look at the sour expressions on our faces!"

Aunt Kei glanced at the picture and let out a snort of laughter. "That's exactly *why* I framed it," she said, settling cross-legged on the floor in front of the bookshelf and holding a plate out for Mom. "We look like we just ate lemons. That was an awful trip."

Mom nodded her head in agreement as she accepted the plate and sat down next to Aunt Kei. "Ooh, this looks amazing."

"Wait, but why was it awful?" Mika asked as she sat back down next to Andy. "We always have so much fun when we travel!"

Mom and Aunt Kei looked at each other and grinned. "Let's just say your mother and I did *not* get along back when we were your age," Aunt Kei said, stabbing a piece of cauliflower with her fork. "Especially compared to you two."

"Why not?" Andy asked, leaning forward.

Mom shrugged. "Oh, just the usual sibling-rivalry issues. We were *so* competitive about every little thing."

"Like in that photo," Aunt Kei said, gesturing with her fork. "See what I'm holding?"

Mika and Andy examined the photo again. Eleven-year-old Karen Taguchi had her arms crossed tightly over her chest, while her big sister Kei clutched a wooden toy with a bright red ball attached to a string.

"That's a *kendama*!" Andy said, pointing. "We have one of those somewhere at home."

Mika nodded. "It was a present from Grandpa," she added, remembering his demonstration of how they could play with the cup-and-ball toy.

"I was so worried that you two were going to end up in a fight over who was better at it," Mom said. "But you just took turns and cheered each other on!"

"Not like us, right?" Kei joked, nudging Mom with her elbow.

Mika stared at them. "You got in a fight over who was better at kendama?" she asked incredulously, while Andy and Jenny laughed.

"We sure did," Mom replied. "Isn't that silly? But like I said, we were competitive about literally *everything*."

"In all honesty, I was afraid your mom was smarter than me," Aunt Kei told them. "She always had her nose in a book, and her grades were perfect. It made me so insecure and self-conscious about my own grades."

"And I was always jealous of my cool big sister," Mom said, smiling at Aunt Kei. "She's always been so artsy and had incredible fashion sense. She also made friends a lot easier than I did back then."

Watching them together now, Mika found it hard to imagine that they didn't get along growing up. Mom had told them some funny stories about their childhood disagreements before, but Mika had still imagined them being as close as she and Andy were. Seeing the photo of their miserable expressions made her realize that she was lucky that her big brother was also one of her best friends.

"When did you stop being so competitive?" Jenny asked, setting her empty plate on the table next to the armchair.

Aunt Kei shrugged. "Sometime in high school, I guess."

"We developed our own interests, joined different extracurriculars," Mom added. "We each became more confident, and then it was much easier to support one another instead of arguing over every little thing."

"That makes sense," Mika said, picking up her fork again. But then she caught Andy giving her a strange look as Aunt Kei and Mom continued to reminisce. "What?" she asked.

Andy blinked and shook his head. "What? Nothing," he replied, turning his attention back to his dinner. Mika frowned, watching him carefully, but his expression had returned to normal.

Still, she couldn't help thinking that her brother had something on his mind.

THE CASE OF THE VANISHING DRESS

SUSPECT	MEANS	MOTIVE	OPPORTUNITY
Julia Miller	No	Yes	Yes
Veronica Duncan	No	No	Yes
Samantha Foster	No	No	No
Jasper Nelson	No	No	Yes

CHAPTER EIGHT
ANDY

"HEY, ANDY? WHAT'S THIS CHART?"

Andy stuck his head out of the bathroom, toothbrush hanging from his mouth. He pulled it out long enough to mumble, "Why are you looking through my stuff?"

Mika stuck her tongue out. "I'm *not*, silly. You're the one who left it sitting out on the bedside table."

She was holding the small "I Love NY" notebook that Andy had bought yesterday in a convenience store, along with a pack of gum and a pen. Andy knew he could take notes on his phone, but carrying an actual notebook made him feel more like one of the old-fashioned detectives in his mystery novels.

Andy finished cleaning up, then joined Mika at the table next to the window. Their parents had left early that morning for meetings, but they still had a few minutes until Jenny was supposed to arrive.

"I'm keeping track of the suspects," Andy explained. "These are the four people we know of so far who might have taken the dress."

Mika tilted her head. "You didn't do this last year when we were trying to figure out the identity of the Masked Medalist!"

"That was different," Andy replied with a shrug. "This is a potential crime with known suspects. And it's a lot like the books I've been reading!"

"Okay, so what does this stuff *actually* mean?" Mika said, pointing. "Means, motive, opportunity?"

"Means is *how*," Andy explained. "You know, *how* did the suspect pull off the crime? What tools or capabilities did they have?"

"You wrote *no* under the means category for all four suspects."

"Yeah." Andy sighed. "Because I don't *actually* know what you'd need in order to make a dress disappear."

"Hmm." Mika went back to studying the chart. "I think I understand motive—it's *why* the suspect would steal the dress, right?"

"Exactly! Julia Miller's motive is that she's starting her own fashion line and Aunt Kei is technically her competition. Veronica Duncan doesn't have a motive that we know of, but she was just picking up a dress for her boss, Jasper Nelson. We're not sure if *he* has a motive, but he is a costume designer and he knows Aunt Kei. When she told us about the dress, Aunt Kei said that there's a secret with the design . . . What's the secret? Maybe that's what he's after—the design, not the dress!"

"Maybe." Mika's brow furrowed. "What about opportunity?"

"That's *where*," Andy told her. "*Where* was the suspect when the crime took place? Julia Miller and Veronica Duncan were at FIT. Jasper Nelson wasn't, as far as we know, but Veronica's his assistant, so that's his opportunity. And it seems like Samantha Foster wasn't there at all—at least, not that we know of."

"There's a lot of stuff we don't know!" Mika said, handing Andy back his notebook. "*Maybe* Samantha *was* at FIT. *Maybe* Jasper Nelson didn't know about Aunt Kei's secret design. *Maybe* the real thief isn't even on this list of suspects!"

"Right—but that's exactly why I made this chart," said Andy. "I'll keep updating it as we learn more information and find new suspects. When we figure out who had the means, motive, *and* opportunity, we'll finally know who the thief is."

Both his and Mika's phones buzzed at the exact same moment. Andy unlocked his phone and saw a new message in their thread with Jenny.

> **JT:** Morning! I'll be there in 5 . . . aaand I've got a surprise for you guys! 😜

"A surprise?" Mika paused, looking at Andy. "Do you think she found the dress?"

"That would be great!" Andy said. But as he tied his

sneakers, a small part of him couldn't help but hope that Jenny hadn't found it quite yet. Trying to solve this case with Mika was the most fun he'd had with his sister in a while.

"I can't believe we're going to see a Broadway show!" Mika said as she waved her arms dramatically. After a late brunch at a restaurant near their hotel, the three of them were back outside the Crescent Theatre—only this time, the doors were open. Jenny stood at the box office window, talking to the ticket seller. Then she turned and headed back to Andy and Mika.

"This is honestly one of the best parts of Mom's job," Jenny said, as she waved three tickets at them. "Sometimes there are fun perks like gifted tickets to her clients' shows!"

"Nice!" Andy said as he took his ticket. At the entrance, he showed it to an older man in a red vest, who scanned the code before motioning him into the building. Once they were inside, a woman handed him a program with a warm smile.

"Enjoy the show!"

"Thank you!" Andy flipped through the program as he followed Jenny and Mika into the lobby. The second and third pages featured the bios of the cast, along with their photos. Andy immediately spotted Samantha

Foster at the top of page two and found a paragraph about Jasper Nelson on page five. He made a mental note to read both of their bios later.

"Wow, it's so pretty!" Mika said in a hushed voice, and Andy looked up. He gazed in amazement as he took in the theater lobby. It wasn't very big, but it was so . . . opulent—that was the best word he could think of. Thick columns reached up to the high arched ceiling where a large crystal chandelier glittered overhead. The floor was covered in a plush red carpet, and a grand staircase that split into two led up to the balcony seats.

Andy looked down at his jeans and sneakers. "Um. I don't think we're dressed up enough for this place."

Jenny laughed. "You're both fine, don't worry about it. This is the matinee. People dress up more for the evening shows."

Looking around, Andy saw she was right. The crowd milling around the lobby was dressed casually, too.

The cousins' seats were in the orchestra section, only seven rows away from the stage. Andy tilted his head back to take in the hall as an usher led them to their row. It reminded him of a movie theater, but it felt like he'd stepped back in time. The hundreds of red velvet seats, the domed ceiling with soft golden lights, and the half circle balconies all looked like something out of a painting. Andy was a little surprised to see that the stage curtains were already open, revealing the set. It looked like a parlor in a Victorian-style mansion, with a giant bookshelf, a table with three high-backed mahogany chairs, and a bay window with luxurious velvet drapes.

"This is so cool," Mika said in a hushed tone as they took their seats.

"Have you guys ever been to a play or musical before?" Jenny asked.

"Well, I went to Mika's school play," Andy said with a grin. "But our middle school auditorium doesn't exactly look like this."

Mika giggled. "Not even close. Oh, but we did go see a play a few years ago, remember?"

"That didn't look anything like this, either," Andy said, and Mika nodded in agreement.

After a few minutes, the house lights dimmed. A hush fell over the crowd, and Andy put on his glasses, eagerly turning his attention to the stage.

He recognized Samantha Foster the moment she stepped under the spotlight. Her red hair was pinned atop her head in an elaborate bun. She wore an off-the-shoulder lavender dress and held her skirt up as she dramatically made her way to the table at the center of the stage.

Next to Andy, Jenny stiffened, and he heard her suck in a sharp breath.

"What's wrong?" he whispered as quietly as possible.

"That dress . . ." Jenny leaned forward, staring hard

at Samantha. "I don't think it's my mom's, but it looks *so* similar!"

"Really?!" In his surprise, Andy had forgotten to lower his voice. He glanced around nervously and sank down in his seat a few inches. Fortunately, no one seemed to have been disturbed. Everyone's attention was focused on the stage. Andy had only gotten a peek of the dress back at FIT when Noah had unzipped the bag. The fabric had been purple, but he thought it was a few shades darker than what Samantha was wearing now.

"It's not *exactly* the same color," Jenny said softly. "And Mom's isn't off the shoulder. But . . . this is *so* weird. They look almost identical!"

Another actor joined Samantha onstage, and he began to speak as Samantha poured tea out of the porcelain pot on the table. Andy barely heard a word the actor said. He was too busy analyzing every detail of the dress. If only he'd seen more of the original! Maybe Aunt Kei had a picture she could show him . . . although she might get suspicious if Andy asked to see it.

Suddenly, a bright flash to his right made him start.

"Sorry, sorry!" Mika hissed, hastily hiding her phone under her leg in a panic. "I didn't realize the flash was on!"

Andy glanced back at the stage. If the flash had bothered the actors, they certainly didn't show it. But someone else had definitely noticed.

"Excuse me, miss?"

Jenny, Andy, and Mika all looked at the usher crouching in the aisle. For a moment, Andy thought the combination of his outburst and his sister's picture-taking was going to get them kicked out of the theater.

"I'm sorry. We have a strict no-photos-and-video policy during performances. I need you to delete that picture, and if you try to take another, I'll have to ask you to leave." The usher smiled kindly, but her voice was firm.

It was dark, but Mika's face was flaming bright red. So was Andy's. "Yes, okay! I'm so sorry!"

Andy watched as she deleted the photo from her camera roll. As the usher walked back up the aisle, he couldn't help but feel disappointed. It would have been nice to have photographic evidence.

"That was *so* good," Mika raved as they left the theater almost two hours later. "Samantha is incredible. That scene where she threw the teapot through the window reminded me of this one part in my school play when I got to throw a plate! It was actually a prop plate, so it didn't break, but this kid, Jake, was in charge of sound effects and he made it sound like it broke a window offstage, and . . ."

As Mika rambled on to Jenny, Andy couldn't stop thinking about the dress. He'd enjoyed the play a lot, but his mind kept wandering back to the unsolved mystery.

"Hey, Andy, over here!"

Startled, Andy looked up and realized he'd wandered down the busy sidewalk in the opposite direction of Mika and Jenny, lost in his thoughts. His cousin waved him over to where they stood near the alley along the side of the theater.

"Didn't we come from that direction?" Andy said, pointing back toward Broadway.

"Yeah, but I want to hang out by the stage door for a few minutes," Jenny said. "Maybe we can catch Samantha when she comes out and ask her about that dress she was wearing."

Andy quickly pulled out his notebook and pen. "Oh, great idea!"

"It's just so strange," Jenny said, leaning her back against the wall. Four people had already lined up in front of them, and Andy saw they all had pens and programs clutched in their hands. "It really looked like my mom's dress . . . It was similar, but I don't think it was exactly the same. Still, it can't be a coincidence, right?"

"Andy had a theory about Jasper Nelson," Mika told her as people continued to exit the theater. "You said Jasper and Aunt Kei went to school together. Maybe somehow, he found out about her secret design, and that's why he had his assistant steal the dress!"

Jenny's face scrunched in thought. "There's no way

he could've made the dress we saw Samantha wearing in just one day, though. And even if he did somehow manage that, why would he ever think he could get away with it when the lead actress in the play is wearing it for everyone in New York City to see?"

Andy had to admit she was right. "Still, it can't be a coincidence, right?" he said. "He went to school with Aunt Kei, Samantha's one of her clients, you said the dress is almost identical, and Aunt Kei said he's a nightmare." Andy sighed, glancing at Mika. "I wish you didn't delete that picture you took. I mean, I know you had to, but it'd be so helpful to have a photo of the dress right now."

Mika gazed at him for a moment, and Andy could see her mind racing. "Hang on . . ." she said, pulling out her phone. "There's a Recently Deleted photos folder—I've used it a few times, when I accidentally deleted a picture and . . . Ha, yes!"

Triumphantly she held out her phone, and Andy and Jenny moved closer. There on the screen was a photo of Samantha, magnificent in the lavender dress.

"Awesome," Andy said, grinning at his sister. "I'm so glad you broke the rules. *Again*."

"Hey, I didn't know it was a rule!" Mika said defensively.

"But they made an announcement saying 'no photography or recording' at the beginning," Andy said.

"Oops. I didn't hear that! I was looking at the stage. Besides, people take photos all the time at our school plays. I feel kinda bad, but I think this is okay because I'm not going to post this picture anywhere."

"Well, you still got a great picture, Mika," Jenny told her cousin, taking the phone and studying it closer. "And, Andy, you're right . . . This can't be a coincidence. This looks even more like my mom's dress than I remembered. See the empire waist, the asymmetrical bottom? And look!" She used her fingers to zoom in on the neckline. "That embroidery is *identical* to my mom's!"

"Jenny, is that you?"

All three looked up to find Samantha Foster gazing at them curiously from the steps of the backstage door. Samantha was wearing leggings and a tan topcoat, but her bright red curls were now in a relaxed ponytail. She was signing programs for the eager people at the front of the line, who stared curiously from Samantha to Jenny, Mika, and Andy.

"Samantha!" Jenny sounded slightly guilty as she quickly handed Mika back her phone. "Hi! I—I can't believe you remember me."

"Are you kidding?" Samantha smiled as she finished signing for her fans and walked down the steps. "You look so much like your mom. I think I would've known it was you even if we hadn't met before."

Jenny laughed. "Mom actually got us tickets to the

show today—you were fantastic, by the way. So amazing! Oh, and these are my cousins, Andy and Mika. They're visiting from LA."

Samantha smiled at them. "Nice to meet you both! I hope you enjoyed it. Would you like me to sign your notebook?"

"No! I mean, you were great in the show . . . but this is for something else." Andy awkwardly hid his notebook behind his back. "You can sign my program if you want!"

"I mean, do *you* want me to?" Samantha said with an understanding smile.

Andy was tongue-tied. Apparently, Mika was too, because her "Sure. Sign his program. You were so good!" came out kind of squeaky.

"I actually wanted to ask about that dress you were wearing in the first act," Jenny said, coming to the rescue.

Samantha arched her eyebrows. "Oh? Did you recognize it?"

Andy and Mika exchanged an excited look as Jenny nodded. "I did! It looks like my mom's design."

"That's because it *is*," Samantha said with a smile. "The costume designer wasn't too happy when I said that I had a better dress in mind for the scene. But once he and the producers saw it, he couldn't argue with me. It's perfect."

"You mean Jasper Nelson?" Andy blurted out.

Samantha looked amused. "Yeah, that's him! Oh,

that's right—Jasper is old friends with your mom, isn't he?" she said to Jenny.

"Yup, they went to school together," Jenny replied. "But hang on . . . Are you saying my mom gave you that dress for the show?"

"Of course she did! What . . . you don't think I stole it or something?" she added with a little laugh, and Andy winced.

Jenny smiled. "No, no of course not. It's just that my mom didn't mention it. And it looks a lot like this one dress she's planning on using in this big presentation she has on Saturday."

"Oh, the *secret* dress." Samantha's eyes lit up, and Andy stared at her intently. "Yeah, Kei showed that one to me when I picked mine up last week. Darker color, slightly different style, right? She mentioned that the secret one has a special surprise to it, but she said she couldn't show it to me until after her presentation. I'm so curious!"

Jenny let out a sigh, and Andy could tell she was as disappointed as him. "Yeah, that's the one! Anyway, the dress looked amazing on you, and we loved the play."

"Thank you all so much!" Samantha gave Andy and Mika a little wave. "It was great to meet you! Have an amazing time in New York City!"

She headed down the street, and Jenny leaned against the wall again. "Well, that's that," she said glumly. "It wasn't the dress after all. I guess we're back to square one."

"Not exactly," Andy said, flipping open his notebook and taking out his pen. Mika peered over his shoulder as he made a few changes to his chart. "If Samantha knows about the secret design, that means Jasper might, too. And she said Jasper wasn't happy about her using one of Aunt Kei's dresses instead of his in the play, right? That gives him—"

"A *motive*," Mika finished, and Andy nodded.

"Exactly."

THE CASE OF THE VANISHING DRESS

SUSPECT	MEANS	MOTIVE	OPPORTUNITY
Julia Miller	No	Yes	Yes
Veronica Duncan	No	No	Yes
~~Samantha Foster~~	~~No~~	~~No~~	~~No~~
Jasper Nelson	No	~~No~~ Yes	Yes

CHAPTER NINE
MIKA

MIKA DECIDED THAT spaghetti carbonara was her new favorite food.

She twirled her fork in the pile of pasta, watching as the bundle of spaghetti grew wider and wider. Crispy little bits of bacon and grated Pecorino Romano cheese coated the noodles, along with a creamy sauce that the waiter had informed Mika was made with eggs.

"Eggs, bacon, cheese, and pasta," Mika said out loud as she twirled. "I could eat this *every* night!"

Andy glanced at her fork and laughed. "There's no way you can eat that in one bite!"

"Wanna bet?" Mika lifted her fork confidently, then paused, eyeing the spaghetti a little doubtfully.

"That's almost half your plate!" Dad said teasingly. "Are you sure you want to finish it so quickly? Savor it!"

"I guess not." Sighing, Mika shook the spaghetti off of her fork and began twirling again. The restaurant Dad had chosen was in the heart of Little Italy. Just like the Crescent Theatre, Marelli's made Mika feel as though she'd stepped back in time. The restaurant was dimly lit, with candles in glass jars on every table, along with checkered tablecloths. Black-and-white framed photos adorned the oak walls, all featuring the smiling faces of famous patrons and people who Mika guessed were a part of the Marelli family.

"Okay, we've been here for twenty minutes, and you haven't mentioned *Tea for Three*!" Aunt Kei said as she speared an olive with her fork. "How was the show? How was Samantha? What did you think?"

Jenny, Andy, and Mika shared a quick glance, and Mika took a purposefully big bite of spaghetti. She looked from Andy to Jenny, recalling the conversation they'd had with Samantha about her dress. She was really glad her mouth was too full of food to answer.

"Samantha was incredible," Jenny told Aunt Kei. "And the play was so amazing. Dramatic, but also pretty funny, right, guys?"

"Yeah, it was really good! I liked the writing," Andy chimed in, while Mika nodded emphatically. "It was so awesome to see a Broadway theater. Thanks for the tickets, Aunt Kei."

"Of course!"

"It was also totally cool to see one of your dresses on a Broadway stage," Jenny said carefully. Mika chewed slowly, glancing from her cousin to her aunt. "You didn't mention that Samantha was going to be wearing one of your designs in the show."

Aunt Kei beamed. "I was wondering if you'd notice! I hadn't planned on it, but Samantha came by for a fitting last week and saw a few pieces from my new collection. I let her talk me into taking one of the dresses. Honestly, I didn't actually think that she'd end up wearing it in the play."

"Because of Jasper Nelson?" Andy blurted out, and Mika nearly choked. She swallowed, reaching for her glass of water.

"We saw Samantha after the show," Jenny explained hastily. "She told us Jasper was the costume designer, and I remembered that you went to school with him. You said he was kind of difficult to work with, right?"

"That's an understatement," Aunt Kei replied. "Talented guy, but it's his way or the highway, you know? I wonder how he feels about Samantha wearing my dress, but she's pretty strong-willed herself. I bet that Jasper— Karen!"

Mika looked up in surprise. Karen Kudo and a tall woman Mika had never seen before were walking toward their table. "I thought you couldn't have dinner with us, Mom!" Mika exclaimed as Dad got up to pull out a chair for each of them.

"Brianna and I finished up our interview early, and

we decided to come meet up with all of you!" Mom said with a smile. "Everyone, this is—"

"Brianna Richardson!" Andy said loudly. "I *knew* you looked familiar! You played in the WNBA *and* in the Olympics for Team USA and now you're one of the best basketball analysts on TV! I saw that you covered the USC–Arizona game last week! And the Michigan–Oregon game before that! Can we call you Bri?"

Brianna pushed her dark hair behind her ear and grinned. "Of course! My teammates all called me Bri. I see you've got a basketball expert here, Karen!"

"You have no idea," Mom said, laughing. She introduced Brianna to Dad, Mika, and Andy before turning to Aunt Kei. "And this is my sister, Kei Taguchi, and her daughter, Jenny."

Aunt Kei smiled at Brianna. "So nice to meet you, Bri."

"Kei Taguchi . . ." Brianna said slowly. "Hold on a second. Are you a stylist?"

Jenny nudged Mika with her elbow. "Mom's getting to be as famous as her clients!" she said in an exaggerated whisper, and Mika giggled.

"Oh please," Aunt Kei said with a dismissive wave, although Mika could tell she was pleased. "Yes, I'm a stylist, but I'm a long way from being famous."

"I don't know about that!" Brianna said eagerly,

pulling out her phone. "I follow Alisa on Instagram—I absolutely love her—and she posted about you yesterday. This outfit is gorgeous!"

She held up her phone so everyone could see the screen. Mika recognized Alisa's sleek blonde bob and signature bright pink lipstick instantly. In the photo, she posed in front of a brick wall. Her suit matched her lipstick perfectly, from the wide-leg trousers to the oversize tuxedo jacket casually draped over her shoulders. A bold multicolor geometric necklace, a matching statement cuff on her right ear, and a pair of futuristic sunglasses completed the look.

"Oooh, Aunt Kei, I *love* that outfit!" Mika said. "Alisa shouted you out in the caption, too? That's so cool!"

"Well, that was nice of her," Aunt Kei said, eyebrows raised. "I have to say, I'm a little surprised."

"Why?" Jenny asked as Brianna put her phone back in her purse.

"Oh, Alisa's a very sweet girl, but she can be . . ." Aunt Kei lifted a shoulder. "Let's just say she's a little bit finicky about the outfits I choose for her. Including that one. She's so creative and likes to put her own twist on things, but I'm glad she was happy with it in the end! If you'd asked me on Monday, I would've told you that she was going to wear something else entirely . . . or find another stylist."

"Well, I can't imagine why anyone wouldn't want to

work with you," Brianna said. "Actually . . . I have this promo shoot with the other analysts from the network before the big game on Friday and I'm sure you're incredibly busy and probably don't have room for new clients, but—"

"If I don't have room for new clients, I don't have a business!" Aunt Kei interrupted with a laugh. "Tell me more about your personal style. What do you like?"

Mika twirled her spaghetti carbonara as Brianna talked to Aunt Kei, but barely heard anything they said. She'd just remembered something, and it was probably nothing . . . but the more Mika thought about it, the more it seemed like a potentially very *big* something.

"Hey," she whispered, and on either side of her, Andy and Jenny leaned closer. "This is crazy, but Alisa was at FIT the same time we were!"

Jenny's mouth fell open. "What? How do you know that? Did you see her?"

"No, but I heard two girls talking about getting photos with her," Mika explained. "You saw them on the security footage—they were the ones who bumped into me with that cart. They were really excited about meeting Alisa and weren't paying attention to where they were going."

"It could be a coincidence," Jenny said, then glanced at Andy and smiled. "Although I think I know what you'll say about that."

Andy had already pulled out his notebook and was scribbling away, and Mika knew he was adding Alisa to the list of suspects.

"Aunt Kei said that she didn't think Alisa was happy with her outfit yesterday," Mika whispered. "Is that enough of a motive for stealing another dress?"

"Maybe," Andy said, nodding.

Mika glanced nervously at Jenny. "Should we tell Aunt Kei?"

Jenny shook her head. "Hey, you promised!" she whispered, giving Mika a pleading look. "It's only Tuesday and we have until Thursday evening to find the dress. And look—Mom's getting another client right now, and Brianna needs an outfit for Friday. Her schedule is even busier than before! She's already stressed, and I really don't want to bring this up to her now."

"Okay, fine," Mika said reluctantly. But as she dug back in to her dinner, she couldn't help thinking what would happen if they couldn't find the dress. Aunt Kei would only have a day and a half to replace the centerpiece of her collection before her big presentation.

Wouldn't it be better to tell her now? Mika knew that nothing she could say would convince Jenny otherwise. And yet, if they didn't find the dress soon, Aunt Kei's presentation—*and* her dream of having her own clothing line—would be ruined.

THE CASE OF THE VANISHING DRESS

SUSPECT	MEANS	MOTIVE	OPPORTUNITY
Julia Miller	No	Yes	Yes
Veronica Duncan	No	No	Yes
~~Samantha Foster~~	~~No~~	~~No~~	~~No~~
Jasper Nelson	No	~~No~~ Yes	Yes
Alisa	No	Yes	Yes

CHAPTER TEN
ANDY

ANDY COULD SEE HIS BREATH in front of him, a little white puff every time he exhaled. He tugged his baseball cap a little lower on his head, grateful that he'd listened to Dad and remembered to pack his winter coat and gloves. Wednesday morning they'd woken up to a light layer of frost on the windows, and the faintest sprinkle of snow falling from a steel-gray sky. The snow wasn't sticking to the sidewalk or the streets at all, but it definitely felt colder than the day before.

Mika stood next to the giant fountain in the center of the plaza, angling her phone, taking photo after photo. Andy stuffed his hands deeper into his coat pockets and gazed at the three buildings in front of them. All three were stately, imposing structures with enormous white columns and gleaming glass fronts.

"Which one of these buildings is Lincoln Center?" he asked Jenny, who stood next to him, her hands tightly wrapped around a cup of coffee.

"All of them!" Jenny replied. "Lincoln Center is actually a complex of buildings. That one straight ahead is the Metropolitan Opera House. Over there is the David H. Koch Theater, which is the home of the New York City Ballet," she added, pointing to the building on the left. "And that one is where we're going—David Geffen Hall. It's the home of the New York Philharmonic, but there are lots of other concerts there, too. Sometimes when an orchestra from another country visits on a tour, this is where they'll perform!"

"Cool!" Andy said. "So, wait . . . is Alisa performing with an orchestra?" He'd only heard a few of the pop star's songs, but they definitely didn't sound like classical music to him.

"No," Jenny replied with a laugh. "The concert hall's not just for that kind of music. Lots of different types of bands and musicians have played here over the years."

Andy watched as Mika jogged a few steps away from the fountain, then turned around to take yet another photo. A dozen or so pigeons took flight, and Andy watched them soar over Mika's head. He'd seen more pigeons the past few days than he'd ever seen in his life. The blue-and-gray birds seemed to be perched everywhere he looked.

"Do you think there's a chance Alisa knew about Aunt Kei's new fashion line?" Andy asked carefully, glancing at Jenny.

Her mouth tugged down at the corners. "I guess it's possible. She was at Mom's office over the weekend. I don't know how much my mom has told any of her clients about her fashion line. She did mention a secret design to Samantha, but there's *no way* she told anyone what makes the design so special," she added, turning to look at Andy. "She really has kept it a secret. She didn't even tell *me* what it is!"

"Hmm." Andy pulled out his notebook and consulted his chart for what seemed like the hundredth time since dinner last night. It was starting to feel like he was at a dead end. He'd marked Jasper Nelson, Alisa, and Julia Miller all down as having a potential motive and opportunity. So far, it was only speculation. Just because each suspect had a reason for stealing Aunt Kei's dress didn't mean any of them had actually done it. What if the real thief wasn't even on Andy's list of suspects?

He sighed, pocketing the notebook. Hopefully, getting more information about Alisa during their investigation at Lincoln Center today would help him narrow down the list.

"I kind of doubt we'll even see Alisa," Jenny said, and Andy glanced up. It was as if his cousin had read his mind.

"I know," he replied, although he secretly hoped they would run into her the way they had with Samantha. "But you said she's rehearsing today, right?"

"Yeah, but not for a few hours," Jenny said. "The tour will take us backstage, so who knows? Maybe we'll get lucky. Speaking of . . ." She glanced at her watch. "Mika! We've got to go! The tour starts in ten minutes!"

"Coming!" Snapping one final photo, Mika hurried over to them. Her cheeks were flushed from the chilly air, but she was smiling. "Thanks for waiting!"

"No problem," Jenny said. Andy stayed silent. They were running out of time. He hoped his sister wouldn't be too busy taking photos today to help them solve the mystery of the missing dress.

As soon as he had the thought, Andy felt guilty. Of course Mika cared about finding Aunt Kei's dress. He had to believe that they would figure this out together.

Half an hour later, Andy was pretty sure this visit was a bust. Not that he wasn't enjoying himself—their guide, a kind older man with thick glasses that magnified his eyes—had begun the tour by taking them backstage. It had been really interesting to hear about the history of the performance hall and all of the concerts and events that had taken place there over the decades.

But as Jenny had predicted, Alisa was nowhere to be seen. Andy pushed aside his disappointment as they entered the concert hall.

"Whoa," Mika exclaimed. "This is so pretty! Excuse me, sir?"

The tour guide smiled down at her. "Yes, miss?"

"Are we allowed to take pictures here?"

He looked pleased. "Yes, and thank you so much for asking! As long as there are no performances going on, you're welcome to take as many photos as you want."

Andy watched as Mika hurried down the aisle with her phone out and at the ready. He and Jenny followed at a slower pace, tilting their heads upward to look around. Both the stage and house lights were dimly lit. The combination of the dark wood-paneled walls and soft golden lights gave the enormous auditorium an almost ethereal feeling. Andy moved as quietly as possible; there was an anticipation to the silence that hung in the air, as if an invisible audience was waiting for the performance to begin.

"Ghosts," Jenny whispered, and Andy glanced at her, startled.

"Wh-what?"

"Empty theaters always feel haunted to me," Jenny explained softly. "Like all the seats are actually filled with spirits or something."

Andy grinned. "I was just thinking the same thing!"

After a few minutes, the tour guide took them up to one of the balconies. While Mika took photos of the stage, Andy gazed at the balconies on the opposite side of the hall. All of the doors were propped open, and in the distance, Andy heard footsteps—a rhythmic *click-click-click* so faint, he couldn't tell if the person was coming closer or getting farther away.

A blur of movement caught his eye just as Jenny's arm flew upward.

"What?" Andy said, turning to look at her. Jenny's eyes were wide as she pointed to the highest balcony closest to the stage on the other side of the hall. Mika lowered her phone and looked, too.

"I know this is going to sound ridiculous," Jenny whispered slowly, "and it's probably because we were just talking about how this place feels kind of haunted, but . . ."

At that exact moment, Andy saw it—in the doorway to the second balcony, a flash of white.

Mika let out a nervous giggle. "Okay, that really did look like a ghost. But ghosts aren't real."

"Listen," Andy said. "Footsteps."

"Ghosts don't have footsteps. Or do they?" Mika said, less sure of herself this time.

The *click-click-click* had grown louder now, as if someone or *something* was moving down the hall, passing every balcony entrance. Andy and Jenny stared at the third balcony, and Mika raised her phone. A moment later—

"There!"

This time, Andy could tell it definitely wasn't a ghost, but a woman with short dark hair wearing a cream-colored dress.

In silence, the three of them turned to watch the fourth balcony's doorway. Sure enough, a few seconds later there was yet another flash of white as the woman passed by. The footsteps slowed, and Andy heard tinkling laughter.

Andy waited, hoping she would reappear. But the laughter quickly faded away.

"Hey, look at this," Mika said slowly. She was staring at her phone. "I don't think it's a ghost, but I got a pretty good picture . . . Take a look at this dress."

She held the phone out, and Andy's mouth fell open in disbelief. On the screen was a zoomed-in shot of the woman with her head turned away from them. She was perfectly framed in the balcony doorway, holding the skirt of her dress up over her ankles as she moved.

"I don't believe it," Andy said. "It looks like the dress Samantha wore in the play! Wait . . ." He turned to Jenny excitedly. "Is that the dress we're looking for? The one that disappeared? Maybe whoever stole it dyed it or something!"

Jenny shook her head, not taking her eyes off Mika's screen. "No, the bodice is slightly different, and so are the straps. I think that's one of my mom's dresses, but it's not possible to dye a dark-colored dress white."

Andy stared down at his notes for a few moments. Then he sighed audibly in frustration.

"What's wrong?" Mika asked.

"I have motive and opportunity for so many suspects," Andy said, pointing. "But I just can't figure out how anyone had the *means* to steal it. I have no idea how someone could actually make a dress disappear!"

"Watching that security footage was like seeing a magic trick," Jenny agreed. "No one actually opened the garment bag!"

"I wonder if someone messed with the video somehow," Mika said. "What do you think, Andy?"

Andy was staring at Jenny. "Magic trick," he said slowly.

Mika's brow crinkled. "You don't actually think it was *magic*, do you?"

"Not real magic," Andy said. His pulse quickened. "A magic *trick*. An illusion. Aunt Kei has been talking to her clients about her collection, and two of her newest clients are illusionists. Maybe she mentioned the secret dress to them . . ."

"The Leons!" Mika cried. "Oh my gosh, you're right! I can't believe we didn't think of them sooner."

Jenny looked amused. "Guys, they weren't even at FIT—at least, not that we know of."

"Yeah, but it's like Mika said," Andy told her eagerly. "The way the dress disappeared *was* like a magic trick.

They might be the only people who knew about the secret design and actually had the *means* to steal the dress!"

"Okay, let's say you're right," Jenny said. "What about motive? *Why* would they want to steal it in the first place?"

"Umm . . ." Andy thought for a moment, staring at the floor. Then his head snapped up. "Aunt Kei literally called the dress an *illusion* when she was telling us about the secret design. If she mentioned it to the Leons, they might want to figure out the secret for themselves or use it in their act or something like that!"

"Didn't Aunt Kei say they're performing tonight?" Mika asked.

"They are." Jenny looked from Andy to Mika, a smile spreading across her face. "Something tells me we're going to see another show!"

CHAPTER ELEVEN
MIKA

TRYING TO CAPTURE the best angle, Mika took at least a dozen photos of Radio City Music Hall's iconic marquee. Beneath the thrill of excitement, she felt a twinge of anxiety that had been growing stronger all day.

Jenny had been putting on a brave face for her cousins, but as time passed, she was clearly becoming more worried about finding Aunt Kei's dress. *She's been dreaming about this for a long time.* Mika couldn't help but remember what Mom had said. They only had one more day! What would happen if Aunt Kei didn't have the centerpiece of her whole collection for her big presentation on Saturday? What if none of the buyers were interested, and her clothing line failed before it had even begun? Jenny would blame herself!

Mika felt awful for Jenny, but she also had her own worries: spring break was halfway over, and Mika still hadn't figured out a theme for her photography assignment! She imagined going back to school on Monday with all of her homework completed except for the one assignment for her very favorite activity.

The really frustrating part was that Mika had taken hundreds of photos over the last five days. But still, every time she scrolled through them hoping a theme would leap out at her, she just saw pictures of New York City.

The lobby of Radio City Music Hall had a grand staircase, golden lights, and ornate artwork adorning the walls. As Mika followed Jenny and Andy up the steps, she marveled at all of the details. She might not have a theme yet, but she was certainly becoming an expert on all the theaters in New York City.

"I've never actually been to a show here before," Jenny said after an usher guided them to their seats. They were in the second row, and Mika twisted around to take in all the rows of red seats spread out behind them. Beyond that, three long balconies rose up in the back of the hall. The sheer size of the place took Mika's breath away. She tried to imagine walking out onstage in front of so many people. The school play had been fun, but Mika couldn't deny experiencing a tiny bit of stage fright—and that was just in their school auditorium!

"Do you think the Leons are nervous?" Mika asked, facing the front again. "You said this is the biggest venue they've ever performed in, right?"

"It definitely is," Jenny said. "But they've done so

many live shows, I'm sure they don't get stage fright anymore. They're probably just excited!"

Mika wondered how many times she would have to perform onstage before she stopped feeling nervous. While Andy flipped through the program, she turned her attention back to her photos. Mika had saved her pictures of the "ghost woman" from Lincoln Center to a separate folder, along with her picture of Samantha Foster onstage in the purple dress. As she scrolled through to the best picture of the woman in the cream-colored dress, Mika blinked.

The woman had *moved*!

For a split second, Mika wondered if maybe something supernatural really was going on. Then she laughed at herself.

"What is it?" Andy asked.

Mika showed him her phone. "I didn't realize before, but when I took those photos of the ghost woman, the camera was on Live mode," she explained. "It's actually viewable as a super-short video. See?"

She held her thumb down on the photo, watching again as the woman pivoted into the frame. Then, quickly tapping her screen, she went to view the video frame by frame. As the woman's face turned away from the camera, Andy leaned closer. "It's funny . . . I thought she had really short dark hair. But it kind of looks like she's wearing a baseball cap or something!"

Mika studied her screen more closely. "You're right," she said. Then the realization dawned. "Hang on . . ." she said excitedly. After dragging the tracker all the way to the very start of the clip, she moved it slowly to the right once again. The woman twirled into the frame, and halfway through the clip, Mika stopped. Her face was slightly blurry, but there was no mistaking that trademark bright pink lipstick.

"I think it's Alisa!" she shout-whispered. On her other side, Jenny leaned over to see.

"You're right!" Andy sounded excited. "I don't believe it—that was her!"

Jenny's eyes were wide. "Wow, that's really cool. I guess it makes sense, though. I mean, that really looks like one of my mom's dresses."

"Aunt Kei gave one to Samantha and told her about the dress with the secret design," Andy said. "If she gave another one to Alisa—"

"Maybe she told her about the secret design, too!" Mika finished. "Do you think—oh no!"

The three of them stared down at Mika's phone, which had suddenly gone black. Mika held the power button down, but the symbol of a battery appeared instead of her home screen.

"Aw, my battery died," she groaned.

"I guess that's what happens when you take a million pictures in one day," Andy said teasingly.

The house lights dimmed, and a hush fell over the crowd. As the usher passed by their row, Mika hastily hid her phone. Maybe it was for the best that her battery had died. She didn't want to get in trouble again, like she had at the play.

As the curtain lifted, Mika expected some sort of grand, spectacular introduction with dancers, music, and lots of lights. Instead, the audience could now see a young man cast in a single spotlight. He was wearing a navy pin-striped suit and sat on a stool in front of a small wooden table.

Mika recognized Benjamin Leon from the You-Tube videos Andy had shown her and she clapped and cheered along with the rest of the audience. For the next few minutes, Benjamin didn't say a word. He pulled a deck of cards from his jacket pocket and shuffled them with a flourish. Then he spread the cards out on the table. The silence in the hall was occasionally broken by a confused giggle as he arranged the cards in an order only he could see. Mika shifted in her seat, wondering how they were supposed to see the trick if they couldn't even see the cards.

Then, without warning, Benjamin let out a cry of frustration and stood, flipping over the table. The crowd gasped, then laughed nervously.

"Um," Andy whispered. "Is it just me, or is the table . . . different?"

Mika stared at the table. Her brother was right. The overturned table had six legs instead of four. And as Benjamin set it upright, she saw it was clearly larger than it had been before.

Benjamin studied the table, apparently as confused as the audience. After a moment, with a sudden and swift movement, he flipped the table over again. Mika gasped—now the table was even bigger, and the wooden legs were painted bright red!

The laughs and cheers grew as Benjamin continued righting the table, scratching his head, then kicking it or flipping it over. Each time, the table was different in some way. Mika watched unblinkingly, not taking her eyes off the table, but she couldn't spot the moment it actually changed.

"How is he doing that?" she whispered to Andy, who looked equally stunned.

"I have no idea!"

Finally, with a loud cry, Benjamin picked up the table—which was now white and rectangular—and hurled it across the stage. The moment it hit the floor, it shattered into dust . . . and in its place was a woman in a bright red pin-striped suit. Standing up from a crouch, she stretched her arms over her head and yawned. The crowd cried out in amazement, and the woman jumped back in surprise, dramatically shielding her eyes from the stage lights and gazing out at them in bewilderment.

"Oh my! Did the show start already?" she asked her seemingly startled brother, and everyone burst out laughing.

Over the next forty-five minutes, Mika forgot all about the missing dress and her photography assignment. Benjamin and Clara Leon were even more entertaining in person than in their videos. They walked through mirrors and emerged on the other side of the unbroken glass, each wearing the other's suit. They dropped a giant bowl of marbles that defied the laws of physics by bouncing higher and higher until each and every one had vanished somewhere up in the rafters. They turned scarves into snakes and handkerchiefs into fluttering doves.

When Benjamin wheeled a tall metal box with a door onstage, Mika wiggled excitedly in her seat. "They did this one in that video you showed me!" she whispered to Andy. "Benjamin made Clara disappear!"

"I know!" Andy sounded excited, too. Mika knew he was thinking about the security footage of the garment bag hanging in the workshop. If anyone could pull off vanishing a dress without opening the bag—or even being in the room—it had to be the Leons!

"Ben, I think we need to get someone in our audience to help us with this trick," Clara announced. "Last time I let you vanish me, I was stuck on top of the Statue of Liberty all night. Great view," she added to the chuckling audience.

"Fair enough," Benjamin replied. "Anyone out there wanna skip the line for the Statue of Liberty?"

This was greeted with more laughter, and a few shouts from volunteers. As the Leons peered out at the crowd, Mika's stomach did a somersault. Before she could talk herself out of it, she thrust her hand high in the air.

"Me! I'll do it!"

Andy and Jenny looked at her in surprise. "Mika! What are you doing?" Andy whispered.

"Volunteering!" Mika whispered back. "Maybe if I'm part of the trick, I'll be able to see how they do it!"

She waved her hand wildly, half hoping the Leons would choose her, half hoping they wouldn't. The moment Clara's eyes locked onto Mika's, her face split into a grin.

"Right there, second row!" she cried, beckoning for Mika to join her.

Jenny whooped and clapped, and Andy said something Mika couldn't hear as she scrambled past him and hurried down the aisle. A buzzing sound, like hornets, filled her ears as she climbed the steps. The stage lights felt as bright and hot as the sun. Turning slowly, Mika faced the audience, and her pulse raced faster than ever.

She was onstage at Radio City Music Hall!

While Clara was talking, her brother rotated the box around so the audience could see all of the sides. Mika barely heard a word. She found Jenny in the second row, smiling encouragingly. Next to her, Andy's eyes were wide, his gaze locked onto her. He looked worried, and suddenly, Mika realized why.

What if the Leons were actually the thieves?

Mika shook off the thought, reminding herself of Andy's chart. Benjamin and Clara had the means, but no clear motive or opportunity. As Benjamin opened the door to the box, Mika swallowed hard. She crossed the threshold and stepped into the dark space, turning to face the crowd one final time. Mika smiled and gave a small wave as the audience cheered. The last thing she saw was Andy's anxious expression.

Then Clara closed the door, and everything went black.

CHAPTER TWELVE
ANDY

ANDY DIDN'T MOVE A MUSCLE.

He stared hard at the box as Benjamin Leon spun it in a final circle. As he did, Benjamin pulled it across the stage to show it wasn't sitting over a hidden trapdoor. Andy still couldn't believe Mika was onstage, much less inside that box. His sister had volunteered to be part of a magic show! While he knew that performing in theatrical productions at school had helped improve Mika's confidence, he'd never expected anything like *this*!

Andy held his breath as Clara pulled open the door . . . and Mika toppled out. Andy gasped before realizing that it was actually a mannequin with black hair, not his sister.

"Whoa!" Jenny cried, and Andy half stood out of his chair. The mannequin wore jeans and a red top, just like Mika! Jenny placed a hand on Andy's arm. "It's just a trick," she said as the crowd cheered. "It'll be okay!"

Still, Andy couldn't help feeling on edge. He knew,

of course, that the Leons hadn't *actually* turned his sister into a mannequin. But he'd been expecting the box to be empty. This was much, much weirder.

"Whoops," Clara was saying as she lifted the Mika mannequin, propping her up against the box. "Well, that's a first. Is our box broken?"

"Maybe?" Tilting his head, Benjamin walked around to the right side of the box. He tapped it, then smacked it, and something white flew out with a flurry.

"Ooh, a dove!" Jenny shouted, ducking her head as it flew out over the clapping audience. Andy leaned back in his chair—but already, the dove had vanished. Had it flown past him? Was it up in the rafters? Was the dove Mika? Their seats were so close to the stage, but now Andy pulled out his glasses so he wouldn't miss anything—near or far. Andy looked around wildly, then shook his head. It was an illusion, obviously. If he hadn't been so worried about Mika, Andy would have laughed along with the crowd. The Leons were undoubtedly excellent performers.

Benjamin and Clara continued to inspect their supposedly broken box. Every time they opened the door, something strange spilled out onto the stage floor—a fishing pole, a bunch of apples, a poster of the Statue of Liberty. With a frustrated sigh, Clara faced the audience and put her hands on her hips.

"Well, folks, I don't know what to say. I'm just not sure where . . . Oh, there she is!"

Andy, Jenny, and everyone else in the crowd turned to stare where Clara was pointing.

"No way!" Jenny cried, and Andy's mouth fell open. A spotlight illuminated Mika, standing in the third balcony, beaming and waving confidently at all of them!

The crowd burst into applause again, most turning around to face the stage after a few seconds. Unlike the rest of the audience, Andy didn't take his eyes off his sister until the spotlight disappeared. Reluctantly, he turned back to the stage in time to see Benjamin pull open the door to the box once again.

"What?" Andy yelped as Mika stepped out, her cheeks flushed pink from laughter. She waved one final time, as the crowd rose to their feet, whooping and cheering. "How did she get there so fast?"

"I'm so glad we found you. *That* would have been a lot of paperwork," Benjamin said, wiping his forehead as he took Mika's and Clara's hands and walked with them to the front of the stage.

"Ladies and gentlemen, thank you so much for coming to our first show at Radio City Music Hall! We love New York!" Clara shouted above the applause.

There was a loud pop followed by a cloud of smoke, and when it had cleared, the stage was empty.

"*That* was incredible!" Jenny exclaimed above the noise of the audience as the curtains drew closed. "I can't believe they picked Mika! Come on, let's go find her!"

Andy followed his cousin down the aisle, but instead of joining the group of people heading back toward the lobby, Jenny led him to a door by the corner of the stage. "I'm not sure if we can get back there, but we can try," she told Andy before knocking.

A moment later, a security guard opened the door. "Passes?"

"We don't have passes, but the Leons, um, vanished my cousin during the show," Jenny explained with a nervous laugh. "Can you help us find—"

"Hey, it's Kei's daughter!"

Clara Leon appeared behind the security guard, her suit jacket slung over her shoulder. Her face glistened with sweat, but she smiled as she waved Jenny and Andy inside.

"Do I really look that much like my mom?!" Jenny asked, and Clara laughed.

"No, it's not that—she has a photo of you on her desk," she explained. "I noticed it the last time we were at her office. I figured that was you in the second row!"

As she spoke, Clara led them down a short, narrow hallway, then into a cozy room with a few overstuffed sofas and a table piled with snacks and drinks. Andy saw

Mika tearing open a bag of chips as she chatted with Benjamin, and he felt a huge wave of relief.

"Mika!"

Mika's face lit up when she saw them. "Hey! Wasn't that *so cool*! I was part of a show at Radio City Music Hall! I can't wait to tell my drama teacher about this."

Jenny gave her a hug. "That was *amazing*, Mika. How'd you get from the balcony to the box so fast?"

Mika pressed her lips together in a sly smile. "Magicians never reveal their secrets," she said, and Clara gave her a wink and a thumbs-up.

"She knows!"

Benjamin chuckled. "I can't believe we picked Kei's niece as our volunteer. That's such a strange coincidence."

"Was it though?" Andy couldn't help asking. "You obviously had a mannequin with Mika's clothes and hair!"

He didn't mean to sound so suspicious, but neither Leon sibling seemed particularly offended. In fact, they exchanged a secretive look that reminded Andy a lot of the looks he and Mika gave each other from time to time.

"Okay, I'll explain *one* of our tricks to you. *That* wasn't a coincidence," Clara told Andy. "We've actually got a bunch of wigs and clothes backstage. Whenever we pick a volunteer, we just make sure the mannequin looks as close to the person as possible before putting it in the box."

Andy frowned. "But the box was already onstage when you picked Mika!"

"When *you* saw us pick Mika," Benjamin corrected him, arching his eyebrows. "We always pick the volunteer before the show even starts. Normally, we pick a kid. You guys know how to have the most fun!"

"Shh!" Clara slapped her brother on the arm. "You're giving all our tricks away! I just said I'd explain *one*. Don't tell anyone, okay?" she added, looking from Andy to Mika. "We did that one on the *Today* show and people are still sharing the video online. We've hit almost five million views!"

"Oh, that's right!" Jenny said. "My mom mentioned you guys were doing the *Today* show. Was that yesterday?"

"Monday morning," Benjamin said. Like his sister, he'd taken off his jacket and rolled up the sleeves of his dress shirt. "It went off without a hitch. We made America's favorite morning show host disappear!"

Monday morning. Andy let out a long, slow breath. The Leons had been on the *Today* show when Aunt Kei's dress had been taken from the classroom at FIT. That meant they didn't have opportunity. There was no way they could be the thieves.

Disappointed to have reached another dead end, Andy grabbed a snack from the table. As he munched on some popcorn, a new thought occurred to him.

Maybe Clara and Benjamin could help him figure out how the thief might have done it. After all, they were still experts when it came to making things disappear.

"I have a question about a . . . hypothetical magic trick," Andy said slowly.

Clara raised an eyebrow. "Ooh, intriguing. What's your question?"

"How would you make something disappear from a garment bag?"

Jenny cleared her throat noticeably but said nothing. Benjamin flopped down heavily on one of the sofas and took a sip of water.

"Is this your sneaky way of trying to figure out how we made your sister disappear?" he asked playfully.

"No!" Andy said, his face warming up. "I'm not, it's . . ." He glanced at Jenny. "I'm trying to plan my own magic trick. I—I want to make a dress disappear from inside a garment bag."

"Nice," Clara said approvingly. "In my opinion, figuring out my own magic tricks is a whole lot easier than figuring out how other illusionists pull their tricks off."

"Oh, not for me," Benjamin said, shaking his head quickly. "I'm the opposite. Which is why Clara plans most of our tricks," he added jokingly, and the others laughed.

"I'm betting that you have a theory about how we

vanished your sister here," Clara said, settling onto the arm of the sofa and smiling at Andy. "What do you think?"

Andy hesitated, looking at Mika. "Well, she didn't leave the box. I guess there had to be a secret compartment or something inside."

Mika raised her eyebrows at him. Recognizing her best attempt at masking a smile, Andy knew he'd guessed correctly.

"What about when you saw her on the balcony?" Benjamin challenged.

"Um . . ." Andy pictured Mika waving up high from the balcony before vanishing along with the spotlight. "Was it . . . a projection?"

He could tell from the way the Leons were smiling that he'd guessed right again.

Jenny looked impressed. "Wow, Andy! Do you know how they did their other tricks?"

"No," Andy said hastily. "I honestly have no idea. Especially the one with the marbles, that one was . . . *impossible*."

Clara took a little bow. "Why, thank you. I'm pretty proud of that one."

"But what if I want to vanish a dress without putting a secret compartment in the garment bag?" Andy pressed. "How would you guys do *that*?"

Benjamin studied him curiously. "Something tells

me that you aren't planning this trick. You saw it some-where, and you're having a hard time figuring it out. Right?"

"Uh, yeah, you're kind of right," Andy admitted. "Someone walked into a room with a dress in a garment bag. They hung it on a hook and left. For five minutes, no one went near the bag or opened it. When the person came back and opened the bag, the dress was gone!"

"Hmm." Clara nodded thoughtfully. "You know, some-times when zooming in doesn't work, you have to zoom out."

Andy blinked. "What do you mean?"

"She means you already looked inside," Benjamin explained. "If there weren't any secret compartments, it's just a normal garment bag. You've got to step back. You know, think bigger."

Clara smiled encouragingly at Andy.

"Maybe the trick started earlier than you think."

MK: Omg. You will not BELIEVE what I did last night!

RJ: Did you forget to wear sunblock to the pool and end up with a ridiculous goggles tan like my uncle? 😄

MK: LOL no!

RJ: Did you eat an entire pizza by yourself?

MK: ROFL not yet!

MK: We went to see the Leon's magic show and when they asked for a volunteer for one of their tricks . . .

RJ: . . .

RJ: OMG STOP

RJ: YOU DIDN'T

MK: I DID!!

MK: I got up onstage at Radio City Music Hall!! I got in a box and they made me disappear! I was part of the show!!!!!

RJ: WOWWWWWWWWW

RJ: That is seriously amazing!!!

RJ: I know you did the school play, but this is like another level of guts! ★

MK: 😊

CHAPTER THIRTEEN
MIKA

"THIS," MIKA ANNOUNCED, "is the best bagel I've ever had."

She took another enormous bite of the hot, chewy bagel slathered in cream cheese. Usually, Mika picked cinnamon raisin and topped it with a flavored cream cheese like honey or strawberry. But Dad had insisted on ordering all four of them everything bagels with plain cream cheese.

"This is your first real New York bagel," he'd said. "While we're here, you *have* to try it the classic way."

Dad and Mom topped their bagels with thin slices of smoked salmon, red onions, and capers, and drank from mugs of steaming coffee. The Kudo family sat in a booth next to the diner's front window so they could people-watch as they ate.

"Jenny's going to meet us at Grand Central Terminal at one thirty," Mom said, checking the retro clock hanging from the wall. "That should give us plenty of time to walk around Times Square first."

"What are you guys up to with Jenny this afternoon?" Dad asked.

Mika swallowed a bite of bagel a second too soon and coughed. She reached for her milk, glancing a little nervously at Andy. They both knew Jenny was going to pick up Aunt Kei's other outfits from the tailor's this morning. And unless the missing dress had miraculously reappeared, they would be spending the rest of the afternoon doing whatever they could to find it before Aunt Kei even realized it was missing.

Andy paused for a split second before answering. "I'm not sure. I guess it depends on whether she has any errands to run for Aunt Kei."

"Well, is there anything you wanted to do that we haven't done yet?" Mom asked as she took a sip of coffee. "Tomorrow night is the basketball game at Madison Square Garden, and then we're leaving Saturday night."

Mika's stomach dropped. She'd been so preoccupied with finding the missing dress that she hadn't even realized how quickly the week was passing by. "I really want to go to B&H," she said at the exact same time as Andy said, "We should go to Heist House with Jenny!"

The siblings looked at one another for a moment. "Maybe we'll have time for both," Mika said cautiously. "The store is really close to our hotel. Where's the escape room?"

Andy pulled out his phone and began to type. A few

seconds later, he held out his phone. Mika could see a red dot labeled Heist House in lower Manhattan.

"Oh, that's not far from Battery Park," Dad told them, leaning closer to see the screen. "You can see the Statue of Liberty from there, Mika!"

Mika perked up at the thought. "Okay! I guess we'll have to see what Jenny wants to do."

"I already told her about the escape room," Andy said. "She said it sounded like a lot of fun."

"Well, she said she'd take me to B&H too," Mika replied. She was starting to get that feeling again—the sense that her brother was annoyed with her for some reason.

"Yeah, but Heist House would be fun for both of us," Andy pointed out. "The camera store is just for you."

Mika set down her last bite of bagel, her stomach suddenly in knots. Karen and Tom Kudo, sensing the potential conflict, eyed their children and a moment of tense silence passed before Mom spoke.

"I really don't see why you can't do both!" she said lightly. "We aren't meeting up again for dinner until seven. That leaves plenty of time."

"That's true," Mika said a little uncomfortably. She couldn't tell her parents that they might not have time to do both, or either, for that matter. Not if Jenny still hadn't found the missing dress.

"There's time for everything if you plan it right," Dad

added. "Think about everything you two saw and did in Tokyo! You're a great team."

Mika tried to smile. "We can go to Heist House first," she told Andy. "Then we'll do B&H afterward if there's time before dinner."

"Okay, that works, I guess," he said, nodding his head slowly. Mika knew it wasn't just her imagination. Something was definitely bothering her brother.

The temperature had warmed, and the Kudos left their coats and scarves at the hotel before heading to Times Square. The blue sky and sunshine seemed to have brought out even more tourists. As they strolled down Broadway, Mika noticed it was definitely busier in the city than it had been earlier that week.

When the pedestrian light flashed white, Mika stepped off the curb with her parents, and—

Splash!

"Eww!" Mika cried, pulling her foot out of the slushy puddle along the side of the street. "Good thing I wore my boots!"

"This New York weather is something. It's really warm today," Dad said, chuckling. "Are your socks still dry?"

Mika shook her foot, gripping Dad's arm for support. "Yup! All good."

Over the next two hours, Mika continued taking photos nonstop. She and Andy posed on the giant red steps in the middle of Times Square while Dad took tons of pictures of them on Mika's phone. They wandered through M&M's World, where glass canisters filled with candies, all organized by color, stretched up to the ceiling. Mika sent a few photos to Riley, who immediately responded: Souvenir, please!!! She purchased a small bag of dark chocolate M&M's in three different shades of green, Riley's favorite color, and tucked it into her bag. They spent twenty more minutes browsing Midtown Comics, where Andy and Mika purchased two comics each to read on the flight home.

While seeing so many different stores was cool, what Mika loved best was simply walking down Broadway and taking in all the sights. Mom pointed out Madame Tussauds, a museum that featured celebrity figures made out of wax. One of the displays out front featured a wax figure of Alisa that looked so realistic, Mika couldn't help snapping a photo to show Aunt Kei later.

"Maybe she'll think we met her," she joked, and Andy gave her a half smile.

Mika bit her lip. Something was definitely going on with her brother. Why was he upset? Was it because she wanted to go to the camera store, or was he worried that they still hadn't found Aunt Kei's missing dress?

At a quarter to one, the Kudos walked to Grand Central Terminal. "I think you'll want a little extra time to take pictures before Jenny gets here," Dad told Mika.

"Pictures of a train station?" Mika asked doubtfully. She enjoyed riding the subway in New York City, but other than the street performers playing instruments or dancing, she hadn't been inspired to take too many photos of the stations she'd seen.

Dad laughed. "It's an iconic landmark! Trust me, it's very photo-worthy."

As it turned out, her dad was right. The moment she looked out at the main concourse, she was met with a view of gleaming marble floors, towering columns, and a high arched ceiling. The information booth in the center of the bustling concourse featured a shiny brass clock with four faces. Over the ticket windows, LED boards flickered and updated every few seconds with information about arriving and departing trains.

"Did you notice the ceiling?" Mom asked, giving Mika a small nudge. Mika shook her head before leaning back to take a look. The arched ceiling was teal blue, featuring an intricate painting all in gold.

"Are those gold lines supposed to be constellations?" Mika asked wonderingly.

"That's right!"

"Wow, it's so beautiful," Mika said as she snapped

away on her phone. "But these would be so much better if I had a real camera," she said with a small sigh.

Mom glanced at her. "A real camera? Isn't the camera on your phone real?"

"I mean, like, a professional camera," Mika said. "A big one with a lens, like the ones they have at school. I know, the equipment isn't as important as the photographer," she added hastily when Mom frowned. "It's just that a big camera can do even more! If I had a wide-angle lens, I think I could get a photo of the *entire* ceiling. And if I had a telephoto lens, I could zoom in closer and get a really clear shot of the details!"

"I guess it might be more challenging in some cases to take a great photo on a phone," Mom said, and Mika nodded.

"Exactly!"

"But why is that a bad thing?" Mom asked. "Challenges are what make artists even better at their craft! If you can't capture the entire ceiling or zoom in on all the details, what *can* you capture? Besides, phone cameras are so good these days. My first cell phone didn't even have a camera."

Mika frowned, considering this before looking up at the ceiling again. Instead of trying to fit as much of the ceiling as she could on her screen, she focused on capturing different sections, while walking slowly across the concourse with Mom. With each photo she took, Mika felt more inspired.

"If I upload these to Instagram in the right order," she told Mom excitedly, "I can show the details and the size of the ceiling on my grid!"

"That's a good idea!" Mom said with a grin. "I love it!"

"Mom! Mika!" Andy called. "Jenny's here!"

After one final photo, Mika hurried over to the stairs, where Dad and Andy stood with Jenny.

"You guys want to grab some lunch?" Jenny asked. "There's a little place nearby that makes fantastic sandwiches."

"Sure!" Andy said, and Mika nodded in agreement. She flipped through the photos of the ceiling on her phone as Mom and Dad made plans with Jenny to meet back at the hotel at six thirty. Once her parents had given them hugs goodbye, Mika turned to her cousin.

"Any news about the dress?" she asked anxiously.

Jenny's face fell. "No. I picked up the clothes from the tailor this morning and brought them to my mom's office. She's super busy with her clients today so she didn't look . . . but I know she has her final fittings with her models for the presentation starting tomorrow morning. I don't know who was supposed to model the special dress, but . . ."

Jenny trailed off, lifting her hands helplessly. Mika felt terrible for her.

"So what should we do now?" Andy asked.

Jenny shook her head. "I think we've done all we can at this point. I'm going to have to tell my mom what happened tonight at dinner. I would tell her now, but she's on location at a shoot and I think I should talk to her in person. Maybe if I tell her in front of everyone, she won't get as mad."

Mika's stomach dropped. "I'm so sorry," she said. "I wish we could've done more to help you find it."

"Are you kidding?" Jenny asked her incredulously. "You guys were amazing! You did your best to help—and on your vacation, too. I owe you both big time. Let's try to go have some fun today. Okay?"

"Okay," Mika said. But she could tell from Andy's expression that he felt as bad as she did.

CHAPTER FOURTEEN

ANDY

HEIST HOUSE WAS ACTUALLY an old fire station that had been converted into an escape room. The small, two-story brick building sat between two taller buildings that were much more modern-looking and made out of glass and steel. Andy took a photo from across the street, making sure the black-and-yellow sign reading HEIST HOUSE was in focus, then sent it off to Tyler.

> **AK:** Here we go! 40 mins or less! 😃

Tyler responded immediately.

> **TS:** You mean 41 mins or more! 😃

"Thanks for doing this with us," Andy said to Jenny as they walked into the lobby. He still felt bad that they hadn't been able to find the dress—at least, not yet. Even though Jenny had decided to tell Aunt Kei what had happened, Andy wasn't going to give up. Ever since the show last night, he'd been turning Clara and Benjamin's advice over and over in his mind and pulling out his notepad to study the suspects whenever his parents weren't looking. If Andy could just figure out the *means*—*how* the thief had vanished the dress—he might be able to figure out their identity, too.

"Of course! This should be fun!" Jenny replied. But Andy could tell she was distracted. So was Mika, with her photos—just like she had been all week. Andy hoped that once they got inside, Mika would see how cool the escape room was and have fun solving it with him.

While a group of teens stood at the counter paying for their room, Andy, Jenny, and Mika hung back and looked around the lobby. Framed photos of fictional newspaper headlines reading things like HEIST OF THE CENTURY! and THIEVES CAUGHT; LOOT REMAINS MISSING! hung on the exposed-brick walls, along with mug shots of the group who had pulled off the supposed heist.

Andy had read all about the theme of the escape room on the Heist House website. "The story is that they broke into a jewelry store and got away with a million-dollar diamond necklace," he told Jenny and Mika, pointing to the mug shots. "They were caught after a long chase, and the thieves claimed they hid the diamonds in this 'house,' but no one ever managed to find them. The only way to win and escape the room is to find the necklace."

Jenny grinned. "So if we find it, can we keep it? I

could definitely use a million dollars. I'm *kidding*, Andy," she added when she saw Andy's expression. "Obviously I know it's fake."

Andy laughed. "I think it's actually pretty ugly," he admitted, pulling out his phone. "There's a picture on their website. See?"

He showed Jenny and Mika, and they both made faces.

"Totally tacky and out of style," Jenny said, and Mika quickly nodded in agreement.

The group of teens headed for the door, and Andy led the way to the counter, where an attendant with a mustache and bright blue eyes smiled at them.

"Welcome to Heist House!" he said in a booming voice, like he was performing onstage in front of a huge crowd rather than standing in a small lobby with three other people. "Decades ago, four diabolical thieves broke into Manhattan's most famous jewelry store and got away with a necklace valued at—"

"A million dollars," Andy finished. "And they hid it here and we have to find it to get out of the room."

The attendant's face fell slightly. "Aw. You know the story?"

"Yup!"

"Want to hear it again?" The attendant cleared his throat, then waved his arms and bellowed, "*Decades ago, four diabolical—*"

"That's okay, we're all set!" Andy said over Mika's giggles.

The attendant winked at him. "Okay, okay. Three?"

"Yes, please," Andy said, pulling out his wallet. That morning, Mom had given him a little extra cash to cover Jenny's ticket to the escape room as well.

"Aw, thanks!" Jenny said, just as her phone began to buzz. Taking a few steps back, she pulled it out and answered. The mustachioed man handed Andy three tickets.

"No portable telephones or moving-picture cameras allowed in the room, so use the safe over there to store all of your precious personal belongings." After Andy and Mika had placed their things in the lockers, he pointed to the entrance for the room and continued. "No food or beverages, and there's a red button right next to the door—just press that if you need to get out quickly. Any questions?"

"Nope, we're ready to go!" Andy said, eager to get started. The man glanced at Jenny, who was still on the phone. When she saw them looking at her, she lowered her phone slightly and whispered.

"You guys go ahead," she said. "I'm really sorry, but I have to take this call."

Andy tried not to let his disappointment show. "No problem!"

The man refunded their third ticket and then guided

them up a narrow staircase that led to a black door. "Remember, the red button lets you out if you can't figure it out!" he said cheerfully, pulling the door open. "And the timer starts as soon as I lock you in. Good luck!"

The door clicked closed behind them, and for a second, they couldn't see a thing. As the lights gradually brightened, a slow tinkling melody came from the player piano in the far corner. Andy's heart raced as he took in their new surroundings. The room was large, at least twice the size of the Kudos' living room at home, with a woven rug in the center of the hardwood floor, a massive stone fireplace, a square table with six high-backed chairs, and portraits of people in old-fashioned clothes in gilded frames.

"I hope Jenny's okay," Mika said, walking over to a bookshelf and examining the books. "She must be so nervous to tell Aunt Kei about the dress tonight."

"Yeah, I know," Andy said. He surveyed the room closely, trying to figure out where to start. A painting of a bowl of fruit hung slightly crooked—could that be a clue? He jogged over to examine it more closely.

For a few minutes, the Kudo kids explored the details of the room separately. The piano switched to a lively waltz and Andy gave up on the painting and moved on to take a closer look at the fireplace. Two dusty candleholders sat on either side, along with a brass figurine of a woman carrying a basket filled with what looked like loaves of bread. Like the painting, the figurine was slightly tilted, and when Andy moved it over, he found a tiny antique key on the mantel. He picked it up and looked around. There were no doors, other than the one they had come in through, and he didn't see any closets or cabinets with a keyhole.

Andy turned back toward Mika. She was still standing by the bookshelf, but her expression was distant.

"Everything okay?" Andy asked.

"Huh?" Mika blinked. "Oh, sorry. This book sticking out from the others is called *Eat Like Royalty*," she explained, pulling the book off the shelf.

"And you think it's a clue?"

"Oh, no," Mika said with a little smile. "I was just thinking that maybe food in New York could be the theme for my photography assignment. I got some pretty good pictures of all the stuff we've been . . . Hey, what's wrong?"

Andy faced the mantel again, trying to hide his irritation. "Nothing," he said. When Mika didn't respond, he sighed and turned around. "Okay, it's *not* nothing. While we're in here, can we just focus on trying to get out of the room so we can beat Tyler's time? I mean, that's why we came here in the first place. Lately, it feels like you don't care about doing things together."

Mika's mouth fell open. "What?"

"Because . . ." Andy instantly felt bad for bringing it

up. But he had to be honest with his sister. "Well, it feels like during this whole trip, you've been more interested in taking pictures than hanging out with me."

"I want to do well on my photography assignment." Mika hesitated. "And I . . . I love taking pictures! There's nothing wrong with that."

"Of course there isn't," Andy said quickly. "It's just that, well . . . last summer, we had so much fun playing *OlympiFan* in Tokyo, *and* we figured out who was sabotaging the game. *And we won!* But when we got home, you weren't really into being a beta tester with me because you got so busy with photography club— which is fine, I guess, but beta testing was supposed to be *our* thing! I guess I just wish things could go back to the way they used to be."

The piano transitioned into a ragtime melody, the tempo gradually increasing with every measure.

Mika swallowed. "I'm sorry, and I think I get it. But maybe it's okay that we have different interests now. I mean, Riley and I are in different clubs at school, but we're still best friends. You and I are still best friends, too . . . right?"

As she spoke, she set *Eat Like Royalty* back on the shelf—but missed. The book fell to the floor, and Mika leaped back as it landed close to her feet. Something small flew from the open pages, hitting the hardwood with a light *clink*.

"What's that?" Andy asked, walking over as Mika knelt down. She held up a tiny antique key, her brow furrowed.

"This key was stuck inside the book!"

"It looks just like this one!" Andy said excitedly, showing her the key he'd found underneath the figurine. "But I don't see any other doors in here, do you?"

"No, but these are really small," Mika pointed out, getting to her feet. "Maybe they open a jewelry box or something?"

Andy considered this. "A jewelry box would be way too obvious of a hiding place for the necklace," he said. "But I bet you're right. These keys have to open *something*!"

The Kudo kids quickly returned to exploring the room for a few minutes, scouring every shelf and surface for anything with a keyhole. The piano music was faster than ever, a low minor chord pulsing beneath the racing melody. Suddenly, Mika let out a cry, and Andy whirled around.

"Did you find it?"

"No, but look!" Mika had opened one of the cabinet doors to reveal a collection of crystal drinking glasses. As Andy joined her, she began carefully lifting and examining each one. When she got to the fourth one on the shelf, she discovered a third key lying underneath.

Andy stared at it, his mind racing. "Three keys," he said slowly. "Why are there three?"

"Maybe whatever the necklace is hidden in has three different locks," Mika said. "But then again, we still haven't found anything with even *one* keyhole."

"Exactly." Crossing his arms, Andy turned around and examined the room again. "We aren't looking for a box, or a door, or anything like that. We need to think about this differently."

Once again, the memory of Clara and Benjamin Leon's words came to mind. *You've got to step back and think bigger.* He felt as if the answer to how the thief had vanished the dress was right in front of him, but he couldn't quite grasp it . . . *yet.*

"Food," Mika said suddenly.

Andy glanced at her. "Are you hungry already? We just had lunch!"

"No, food might be the thing that links everything together!" Mika pointed to the glasses. "We found this key in a cabinet filled with glassware, and I found the other key in a book about food. Where did you find your key?"

"That figurine on the mantel," Andy said. "Of a woman holding a basket of . . . bread! You're right! Food definitely has something to do with it—the painting!"

He hurried back to the slightly crooked painting of the bowl of fruit, Mika right on his heels. With some effort, Andy shifted the heavy frame up, fully expecting to see some sort of safe hidden in the wall. There was nothing there.

"I don't get it. There's got to be—" His words were cut off by another clinking sound as something landed next to his foot. Andy knew what it was even before Mika said it.

"Another key!" She scooped it up and held it out. "It must have been on top of the frame!"

"Four keys, but no keyholes," Andy said, squeezing the key in his palm. He glanced at the timer on the wall: they'd been in the escape room for almost half an hour already. It was crunch time. Less than ten minutes to go if they were going to beat Tyler's record. The piano melody had reached an incredible tempo, only increasing the sense of urgency.

Food. The figurine with the bread, the painted bowl of fruit, the glasses, the book. Mika was right—food was definitely the theme here. Wherever the necklace was hidden, it was probably in a food-related place. The only problem was, Andy didn't see anything like that here. There was no refrigerator, no stove, no pantry . . .

Andy's gaze fell on the table.

"Mika," he said slowly. "Look at the chairs around the table."

He walked toward the table as he spoke. Mika joined him, frowning. "What about the chairs?"

Andy pointed. "Six chairs, but it's a square table. These two pairs are crammed close together. If anyone actually tried to sit in them . . ."

"There would be no room. It'd be hard to eat," Mika said, finishing his thought. "Your elbow would keep bumping into the other person."

"Right!" Andy examined the table. It was heavy and solid, with a thin crack running down the center. "Look at this."

"That's probably where the leaf goes," Mika said.

Andy looked at her, confused. "The leaf?"

"Yeah! Riley's dining room table has one," Mika explained. "It's an extra piece for the table that you can put in to make it longer."

"Oh. *Oh.*" Andy felt a familiar zinging sensation up and down his spine. It was the feeling he always got right when he was on the brink of solving a puzzle. "Maybe this table is supposed to be longer! If we had the leaf, how would we put it in?"

"Umm . . ." Mika pulled one of the chairs out of the way and felt underneath the table. "I saw Riley's parents do it once. They stood on opposite sides of the table and pulled it apart."

"They just pulled it?" Andy said, bewildered.

"Yeah, but I think they had to adjust something underneath the table first."

Andy moved to the opposite side of the table and

crouched down. Rather than four legs, this table had one center leg, a thick column that didn't quite touch the underside of the tabletop. In the shadows, Andy could barely make out metal bars and gears, along with . . .

"A keyhole!"

"There's one here, too!" Mika shouted. "And I bet there are two more on the other sides!"

She pushed one of her three keys across the table to Andy, who snatched it before quickly ducking back down. He inserted one of the antique keys in the keyhole and twisted. It turned with a satisfying *click*.

Once all four keys were in, Andy and Mika pulled the rest of the chairs out of the way. They stood on opposite sides of the table so the crack ran parallel between them.

"Ready?" Andy said.

Mika grinned. "Ready!"

Together, they both gripped their edge of the table and pulled hard. A trill came from the highest keys on the piano, and Andy held his breath. With a loud *creak*, the gears beneath the table began to turn, and the two halves came apart about two feet, exposing the top of the column.

Resting gently on its surface was the diamond necklace.

"We did it!" Mika cried, right as a trumpet fanfare blared through the speaker next to the timer. The piano tune ended on a low, dramatic chord, fading to silence.

Andy turned to see where the time had stopped.

"We figured it out in only thirty-six minutes!" he exclaimed, grinning at his sister. "We really *are* a good team."

Mika beamed. "Definitely."

"Listen, I'm sorry if I've been acting kind of weird. I should have just told you how I felt about everything when it was bothering me," Andy said as they headed back toward the door. "It's pretty awesome that you're so into photography club. I guess I just missed doing things together like we did during the summer. But you're right—it's okay that we like different stuff now. Maybe it's even a good thing. I mean, Mom said that's why she and Aunt Kei finally started getting along when they were younger."

"As long as we're still best friends," Mika said tentatively. "We are . . . aren't we?"

"Yeah. Of course we are!"

Andy pulled open the door, and the two of them hurried down the stairs. He could hardly wait to get his phone back so he could text Tyler. However, when they reached the bottom of the steps and saw Jenny, Andy knew something was wrong.

"Thank goodness you guys are quick at solving things. I was just going to try and break you out of that room myself," Jenny said breathlessly. "You aren't going to believe this. Noah called—he found the dress!"

"What!" Mika exclaimed. "That's great news! Where was it?"

But Andy noticed that Jenny didn't look too excited. In fact, she looked worried.

"That's the thing. He doesn't actually *have* it." She paused as she unlocked her phone, then held it out so they could see a photo. The image was slightly blurry, but after a moment, Andy realized the camera had been held close to a pane of smudged glass. It looked like one of the classrooms at FIT . . . and in the center of the room was a mannequin wearing a familiar purple dress.

"The door is locked, so Noah can't get to it," Jenny said grimly. "But that's Julia Miller's classroom. I think we just found out who stole my mom's dress—and we have to get it back."

AK: Hey. Just got out of Heist House . . .

TS: And?

AK: . . .

TS: What happened? How long did it take??

AK: . . .

TS: C'mon man!

AK: 36 MINUTES! Heist House has a new record holder!

TS: Noooo!

AK: 😃

TS: Haha I figured you guys would do it. Good job! 👍

AK: It was really cool. Thanks for the rec!

THE CASE OF THE VANISHING DRESS

SUSPECT	MEANS	MOTIVE	OPPORTUNITY
Julia Miller	No???	Yes	Yes
Veronica Duncan	No	No	Yes
~~Samantha Foster~~	~~No~~	~~No~~	~~No~~
Jasper Nelson	No	~~No~~ Yes	Yes
Alisa	No	Yes	Yes

CHAPTER FIFTEEN
MIKA

"BUT HOW?" ANDY SAID for what seemed like the millionth time after they left Heist House. "*How* did Professor Miller make the dress disappear?"

Mika glanced at her brother. His eyes were glued to his notepad as he tried to keep up with the brisk pace Jenny had set. She hadn't said a word since they exited the bustling subway a few minutes ago, but Mika could tell Jenny was still stressed from how tightly she was gripping her hand.

For good reason. Mika's stomach churned uncomfortably at the thought of confronting a professor and accusing her of stealing. But then again, Aunt Kei's dress was in her classroom! What more proof did they need?

Noah was waiting for them in the lobby. If possible, he looked even more anxious than Jenny. "Good timing," he said when they reached him. He continued talking as he led them to the elevators. "A few minutes after I sent that picture, Professor Miller showed up with some of her students."

"Did you say anything to her?" Jenny asked.

Noah shook his head quickly. "I didn't want to accuse a professor of stealing something in front of her students."

The four of them stepped into the elevator, and Noah pressed the button for the second floor.

"Is she teaching a class right now?" Mika asked.

"Yes, but it started about forty-five minutes ago," Noah said. "They should be done any minute."

Mika exhaled and looked at Andy. He was staring at Noah, his brows pulled together tightly the way they always were when he was deep in thought. When the doors slid open, Mika waited for Noah and Jenny to leave first, then stuck close to her brother's side as they walked.

"What is it?" she whispered.

"The trick started earlier than we thought," Andy whispered back.

Mika frowned. "What?"

"That's what Clara said, remember?" Andy slowed slightly, putting more distance between them and Jenny and Noah. "We know that when Noah left us, the dress was in the garment bag. And on the security footage, we saw him carrying it when he walked into the classroom. But what about the time in between?"

"Hang on." Mika stopped, grabbing her brother's

arm. "You're not saying Noah took the dress, are you?"

"Well . . ."

"But he's Jenny's friend!" Mika said in a hushed voice. "Besides, what would his motive be?"

"I don't know," Andy admitted. "But—"

"And why would he put the dress in Professor Miller's classroom, then text Jenny a picture of it?" Mika added.

Andy sighed. "Maybe he's trying to frame her. You know, make us think she did it . . . I don't know. It doesn't really add up and I guess Jenny trusts Noah."

But Andy didn't look entirely convinced as they continued down the hall. Jenny and Noah stood outside a door with a small rectangular window and a sign that read 205. Mika peered inside and drew a sharp breath when she spotted a purple dress. With all of the students milling around as they put away fabric and other supplies in the cabinets, it was hard to get a good look.

"Here they come," Noah said, taking a quick step back from the door. Jenny, Mika, and Andy moved to stand against the wall as the door opened and students began filing out. Most of them carried books or backpacks, but none walked out with a garment bag. When the last student had left, Noah caught the door with his foot before it closed. He held it open for the others, then followed them inside.

Mika was filled with excitement when she spotted the dress. Aunt Kei's presentation was saved! But as she drew closer, her relief turned to confusion, then worry.

Something was *very, very* wrong.

"Hi, Noah! Can I help you?" Professor Miller glanced up from where she sat behind the computer at her desk. Mika hung back and closely examined the dress. The shimmery fabric was purple, although a touch darker than Mika remembered, and the embroidery around the neckline was identical to the dress Samantha Foster had worn in the Broadway show. But the skirt hung in jagged pieces with the seams exposed, and on the back, Mika could see only half of the tiny pearl buttons had been sewn on.

"Hi, Professor Miller," Noah said. "This is my friend Jenny, and these are her cousins, Andy and Mika."

Mika stepped away from the dress as Professor Miller smiled around at them, clearly trying to hide her confusion. "So nice to meet you all."

"Jenny is Kei Taguchi's daughter," Noah went on. Mika watched as Professor Miller's face lit up and she got to her feet.

"Is that right?" she said, shaking Jenny's hand. "How lovely to meet you. I'm a big fan of your mother's work."

"Thank you, I'm actually here because, well, that dress over there is—" Jenny said nervously, and Mika's pulse quickened. She had to say something.

"Not finished," Mika interrupted. She felt her cheeks flush as all heads turned in her direction. "It's not finished," she repeated, pointing at the dress. "I don't think that dress is Aunt Kei's, Jenny."

"What do you mean?" Jenny asked, turning away from Professor Miller.

Mika watched as she and Andy hurried over to take a closer look. After circling the mannequin, Jenny's shoulders slumped in disappointment.

"You're right," she whispered. Then she turned as Professor Miller and Noah approached.

"What's going on?" Professor Miller sounded bewildered.

"This dress . . ." Jenny gestured to the mannequin. "It looks a lot like one my mom designed. I gave it to Noah on Monday to fix a tear, and it disappeared."

"Disappeared?" The teacher looked more confused than ever.

"Yes, right here in this classroom!" Noah added. "We talked to Ricky over at campus security and watched the footage. I hung the dress in a garment bag right over there," he said, pointing to a hook near the door. "Then I went down the hall to grab a coffee, and when I came back . . . the bag was empty!"

Next to Mika, Andy's head jerked up. She glanced at him, but he wasn't looking at Noah. He was looking at the table with the sewing machines and all of the different rolls of fabric.

"How odd," Professor Miller said. "This dress here

belongs to one of my students, Tina Shah." Stepping forward, she touched the neckline. "I think it's a personal project she started earlier this week. Tina intended to finish yesterday, but it's been giving her a hard time."

"I don't understand." Jenny rubbed her temples with her fingers. "This can't be a coincidence, right? Mom's dress goes missing in this room on Monday, and another student starts sewing a dress that looks a lot like it?"

As she spoke, Mika quietly took out her phone and stepped back. She began to take pictures of the dress as Jenny, Noah, and Professor Miller continued to discuss what might have happened.

Lowering her phone, Mika turned to her brother. Deep in thought, he was still staring at the table of sewing machines.

"What's up?" Mika asked.

Slowly, Andy took his eyes away from the table and turned to look at Noah.

"The rolls of fabric!"

CHAPTER SIXTEEN

ANDY

EVERYONE IN THE ROOM stared at Andy as he kept his eyes on Noah.

"What about the fabric?" Noah asked, shrugging his shoulders.

"On the security footage, when you walked into this room, you were carrying Aunt Kei's garment bag with the dress, *and* a bunch of rolls of fabric," Andy said excitedly. "You hung the bag up and set the rolls down on that table over there with all the sewing machines. When we met you in the lobby, you didn't have anything else with you!"

"Oh, right!" Mika exclaimed. "Noah, that means you didn't bring the dress straight here."

"You stopped somewhere else first," Andy said. "Where did you get the fabric?"

Noah's expression cleared. "Oh yeah, I swung by Professor Abrams's office to pick them up for my project. But I know I had the dress with me the entire time."

"Are you sure about that?" Andy pressed. "Did you put the garment bag down somewhere, even for a second?"

"No. I don't think . . . Wait, hold on. Actually . . . yes!" Noah frowned slightly. "I hung it up by the door so I could pick up the fabric, but I wasn't in there for more than a minute."

Andy's heart was racing now. "Do you think there's security footage of the hallway outside of Professor Abrams's office?"

Five minutes later, Andy, Mika, Jenny, and Noah were back in the campus security room with Ricky. He was chuckling as he scrolled through the security camera files.

"I have to say, I'm glad you kids are still on the case," he said. "It's been driving me nuts . . . The Case of the Vanishing Dress! Dun-dun-dunnnnn." He raised his eyebrows and looked around at each of them, but his playful smile was only met with strained looks from the group.

"Jeez . . . Tough crowd. All righty, then. Let's take a look . . ." Ricky sat back so everyone could see the screen. "This is the closest camera to Professor Abrams's office. Which is that door there," he added, pointing.

Andy focused all of his attention on the screen. The time stamp in the corner read *09:32 a.m.* Professor Abrams's door was closed. This hallway was fairly busy as students filed in and out of classrooms. At the end of the hall, Andy could just make out the elevators. The doors slid open, and Noah stepped off, followed by a man pushing a cleaning cart.

"That's me," Noah said, pointing at the screen. The five of them watched as he carried the garment bag with Aunt Kei's dress down the hall, then hung it on a hook outside the door before knocking. A moment later, Noah stepped inside the office, closing the door behind him.

The room was utterly silent as everyone watched and waited. Andy's eyes stayed glued to the man pushing the cart down the hall. The silence was only broken when Ricky took a loud slurp from his coffee mug. Everyone jumped, but quickly reverted their attention to the screen. Suddenly, another cart with at least a dozen garment bags came into view heading up the hall—fast. The cart was being pushed by two girls who seemed distracted, talking excitedly and laughing about something. Mika murmured under her breath, but Andy barely heard her.

Before they knew it, the two carts had clipped each other, and Jenny gasped as the cart with the hanging garment bags teetered precariously before tipping toward the wall. One girl leaped out of the way while the other tried to balance their cart, but it was no use. The cart, top-heavy from the garment bags, toppled over . . . pulling Aunt Kei's garment bag off the hook.

"I can't believe I didn't hear any of that," Noah

whispered as they watched the chaos unfold on the screen. "Professor Abrams and I were talking about my project, and . . ."

Noah trailed off, watching as the man helped the two girls collect and hang their garment bags back up. Andy held his breath. He knew what would happen a moment before it did.

The man picked up the last bag and hung it back on the hook on the wall. Then the two girls smiled sheepishly and waved before continuing down the hall to the elevators. Next to Professor Abrams's office, the man pushed his own cart into the restroom, and a second later, the office door opened, and Noah stepped out with an armful of different-colored fabric. A lanky, gray-haired man who Andy guessed was Professor Abrams followed him out, taking the garment bag off the hook and laying it on top of the fabric rolls. Noah tilted his head appreciatively, appearing to thank him, and walked down the hall while Professor Abrams returned to his office.

As Ricky paused the footage, Andy blurted out, "So that guy who helped the girls hang everything up hung the wrong bag back on the hook. Which means—"

"Those two girls have my mom's dress," Jenny finished breathlessly.

"Case *closed*!" Ricky said triumphantly, holding his hand up to Andy for a high five.

Andy hesitated before slapping his palm out of obligation. "Well, yeah. Sort of. We still don't know where the dress actually *is*."

Ricky lowered his hand sheepishly. "Oh. Good point."

Jenny turned quickly to Noah. "Do you know who those girls are?"

"That is *exactly* what I was about to ask," Ricky interjected.

Noah glanced at Ricky before shaking his head slowly. "I don't think they're students."

"They're not," Mika said, and everyone turned to look at her. She was looking right at Andy and smiling. "I know them."

"You do?" Andy said in disbelief. "How?"

"When you and Jenny left FIT the other day, I stayed inside for a few minutes to take a video of the lobby, remember?" Mika asked. "You saw the security footage when I was leaving. Those two girls—"

"They were the ones who bumped into you!" Andy cried, remembering. "You dropped your phone!"

"Right!" Mika said. "Those were the girls who were so excited about meeting Alisa."

"But how do you know who they are?" Jenny asked. "Did you get their names?"

Mika shook her head and started to walk toward the door.

"Nope—not their names, but I saw their shirts . . . They work at Zoey's Thrift Shop."

CHAPTER SEVENTEEN
MIKA

THE THRIFT SHOP WAS ONLY a few blocks away from the campus. Mika's thoughts were racing almost as fast as her legs hustling down 27th Street. Noah had told them that students and teachers at FIT often donated clothes there after projects were completed. For the last three days, Aunt Kei's dress had been at Zoey's Thrift Shop.

But would it still be there? And if it wasn't, what then?

Jenny came to a halt outside the shop, rubbing a stitch in her side as she pulled the door open. Bells hanging overhead jingled as she hurried inside, followed by Mika and Andy.

The space was surprisingly large, and the checkered floor was crowded with racks of clothes. Mika scanned the room, her eyes darting from rack to rack, hoping to spot the dress. It would take them forever to search the entire store!

"Excuse me?" Jenny said, and Mika saw her approaching a Black woman with braids wound up into a bun, standing over a box of clothes and studying a clipboard. She glanced up, smiling.

"Hi there! Can I help you?"

"I sure hope so," Jenny replied with a nervous laugh. "On Monday, two girls who we think work here picked up some donations from FIT."

"Oh, yeah, Layla and Viv," the woman said, nodding. "That was a huge donation—as you can see, I still haven't gotten everything on the racks! I'm Zoey, by the way."

"So this is *your* store. It's amazing! I can't believe I haven't been in here before. Nice to meet you," Jenny said brightly. "I'm Jenny, and these are my cousins, Mika and Andy. We're here because one of the dresses that was donated—well, it wasn't supposed to be."

"It got mixed up with another garment bag," Mika explained. "It's kind of a crazy story, but it was an accident."

"I see," Zoey said. "I'm sure we can find it. What does it look like?"

As Jenny began describing Aunt Kei's dress, Zoey's smile slowly started to fade. Noting this, Mika grimaced as she braced herself for more unfortunate news.

"I'm so, so sorry," Zoey said. "I know exactly which dress you're talking about. Unfortunately, someone bought it yesterday."

Jenny's mouth fell open in stunned silence.

Andy jumped in. "But . . . but can't you just ask them

to return it? It wasn't supposed to be a donation!"

"Or can you at least tell us who bought it?" Jenny asked. "We can explain what happened to them!"

"I'm afraid it's against our store policy to give out customer information," Zoey said sympathetically. "I truly am sorry that I can't help you out more."

"It's okay," Jenny said, bravely attempting a smile. "I appreciate it. Thanks anyway."

As they walked away, Mika could tell Jenny was not okay at all.

"There's got to be something else we can do. We've come so close!" Andy said.

Jenny sighed resignedly. It looked like she was about to cry. "There is. And it's what I should've done in the first place. I have to tell my mom what happened."

Rows of lights and ornaments hung from the windows of the dim sum restaurant in Chinatown that Aunt Kei had chosen for dinner. Mika's stomach grumbled as a server delivered a tray loaded with bamboo baskets to their table. She watched as the basket lids were lifted and steam swirled into the air to reveal *shumai, har gow,* and *xiaolongbao.*

"I know that most of the time, shumai has pork and mushroom inside," Mika said, loading up her plate. "And har gow has shrimp . . . but what's xialongbao again?"

"Soup dumplings!" Dad said excitedly, rubbing his hands together. "My favorite! Be careful though, the soup inside is very hot, so don't burn your tongue!"

"Ooh, yum. I'll be careful!" Mika plucked two of the delicately wrapped dumplings from the basket, and then offered them to Jenny. Her cousin didn't seem to notice. Her eyes were glazed over as she stared vacantly into space.

"Jenny! Food!"

"Oh, thanks, Mika. Looks good," Jenny said, blinking in surprise before helping herself to a few as well. However, minutes later, she still hadn't taken her first bite.

"Tell her," Mika whispered, lightly nudging Jenny with her foot. Across the table, Mom, Dad, and Aunt Kei were deep in discussion about an interview Mom had conducted that afternoon. "You'll feel better once you just get it over with. Trust me, I'm speaking from experience."

"Right." Jenny took a deep breath and shifted in her chair. "Sorry to interrupt . . . Mom? I—I have to tell you something."

Mika set down her chopsticks, and on her other side, so did Andy. Aunt Kei looked mildly surprised, as did Mom and Dad.

"Well, this sounds a little serious," Aunt Kei said. "What's going on, Jen?"

Jenny lifted her chin. "On Monday morning when I

was packing everything up to take to the tailor's, I accidentally ripped one of the dresses. *The* dress. The one you said was the centerpiece of your collection."

Aunt Kei's eyebrows rose. "Oh . . . ?"

"I should have told you right away, but I thought maybe if I could fix it first, you'd never have to know. You were already *so* stressed out," Jenny went on in a rush. "My friend Noah said he could fix it that day, and you were busy with work, so we left it with him at FIT, just for a few hours. But then . . . Well, it disappeared! It's a long story, there was a mix-up and the dress ended up at a thrift shop so we tracked it down—but when we got there, someone had bought it and . . . and now it's gone."

Jenny's voice broke on the last word, and Mika felt so bad for her cousin. She glanced nervously at Aunt Kei, who still looked more bewildered than anything else.

"That's quite a story, but I think I understand," she said slowly.

"You two knew about this?" Mom asked Mika and Andy, setting down her glass of iced tea.

"Why didn't you say anything?" Dad added.

"They did know, but it's really all my fault," Jenny said quickly. "I made them promise not to say anything. Mika actually told me on Monday that I should just come clean and tell Mom, but I really didn't want to stress her out more. It felt like I failed as an assistant, and I wanted to fix it myself. I should've listened to you, Mika," she added, pulling Mika into a side hug. "You were right. It's better to be honest from the beginning."

Aunt Kei sighed. "Yes. It would have been much better. I might have been able to come up with a substitute by Saturday if I had known and had the whole week. But now . . ."

"I'm so, *so* sorry, Mom," Jenny said miserably. "I don't blame you for being mad at me."

Aunt Kei reached across the table and took her daughter's hand. "I'm not mad," she said. "I really wish you had told me earlier, but I also appreciate that you were trying to help me out."

"Aunt Kei?" Mika asked timidly. "What about the dresses you made for Samantha Foster and Alisa? They look a lot like the centerpiece dress—could you get one of those back just for Saturday and use it for the presentation?"

Aunt Kei smiled. "They do look similar, but that dress has a secret to the design. It's a prototype—the only one like it that I've made so far."

"Can you tell us what the secret is?" Andy asked.

"I can do better than that." Reaching down beneath her chair, Aunt Kei pulled a thin binder from her bag and cleared some space on the table. "I'll show you guys the design."

Mika and Andy leaned forward as Aunt Kei flipped

the binder open, then turned it around so everyone at the table could see. On the right page was a sketch of a woman wearing the dress—Mika recognized the embroidery along the neckline. At the top of the left page was a sketch of the dress pattern, with strips and squares of fabric all spread out in a way that Mika couldn't quite make sense of. Below that were smaller sketches of a woman wearing the same dress, but each was slightly altered in some way: a shorter skirt, a different waistline, various straps and sleeves.

"That's all the same dress?" Andy asked in amazement.

Aunt Kei nodded proudly. "That's right! See the pattern here?" she said, pointing to the top of the left page. "It took me months to conceptualize and perfect this design. It works almost like origami—the way you can fold a single piece of paper into all sorts of different shapes."

"An origami dress!" Mika cried. "This is such a cool idea!"

"Very innovative," Dad said, looking impressed.

"Sustainable, too," Mom added. "It's like getting seven dresses in one!"

Groaning, Jenny threw her head back. "Ugh, man, now I feel even worse. This would've blown away all of those buyers on Saturday!"

"It's okay, honey," Aunt Kei said, closing her binder. "Maybe I can still show them the design."

"But a demonstration would've been so much more epic!" Jenny said, lowering her eyes. Mika didn't want to make her cousin feel worse, but she silently agreed. Having a real model show off the way the dress could transform, right there in the room, would have made Aunt Kei's presentation totally next-level.

"I'm sure the buyers are still going to be wowed," Mom said reassuringly.

Aunt Kei nodded in agreement. "It's going to be just fine, Jen. You and I can talk more about this later," she said, pushing a platter of pork buns across the table. "Now, can you please eat something already? This delicious food is getting cold!"

Jenny smiled half-heartedly as she picked up her chopsticks and finally started to eat. Still, she remained mostly quiet for the rest of the meal.

So did Mika. As she sampled the shumai, she couldn't help wishing they knew who had bought the dress from Zoey's Thrift Shop. Did that person even realize how unique and special the outfit they'd purchased was?

On Friday morning after breakfast, Jenny took Mika and Andy to B&H. The famous camera store was even bigger and cooler than Mika had imagined.

The building took up a large chunk of the block, its green awnings on the first and second floors stretching all the way down 9th Avenue. Inside, Mika marveled at the elaborate conveyor-belt system running overhead, transporting all sorts of products and equipment to different areas of the enormous store. Everywhere she looked there were displays of different cameras, lenses, lighting equipment, microphones, computers, games, and even drones.

"Where do you want to start?" Jenny asked, taking a sip from her smoothie. She had taken Mika and Andy to a nearby bodega for breakfast burritos that morning before walking to the store.

Mika felt a little dazed as she stared around at the seemingly endless rows of racks and shelves. "I have no idea."

"What about there?" Andy pointed to a display of massive lenses, and Mika laughed.

"Those are telephoto lenses! Photographers use them to take pictures of things really *really* far away."

"Oh, I see some photographers using those when I watch basketball. I bet that one could take a picture of someone walking on the moon," Andy joked, hurrying over to examine one of the largest lenses in the display.

Mika and Jenny walked to the nearest display of DSLR cameras. "That one looks like the one I use at our school," Mika said, gesturing to the one closest to Jenny. "I love it. Ooh, but look at this one!"

She moved from one camera to the next, reading

the descriptions accompanying each one. Mika had learned about a lot of technical photography terms like *aperture, shutter speed,* and *ISO.* But as she examined each camera, Mika started to realize just how much more she had to learn. It was exciting, but also a little intimidating.

"This is a seriously cool hobby, Mika," Jenny said, peering through the viewfinder of a camera and toying with the lens. "You said you're saving up to buy one of these, right?"

"Yeah . . . I have a long way to go." Mika laughed and leaned over to study the price tag of another camera. "But maybe that's okay."

Jenny glanced at her. "What do you mean?"

Mika thought about it for a few seconds before answering. "I really wanted to bring one of the nice cameras from school for this trip," she explained. "I thought my photos would be so much better, and that it would help with my assignment for photography club. But Mom and Dad said that good photography is about the artist, not the equipment, and that using the camera on my phone would be a good challenge for now."

Jenny was nodding in agreement. "Yeah, totally. I can see that. Someone can have the greatest camera in the world, but that doesn't mean they can take a great photo. Just like having a super-nice laptop doesn't make you a better writer, or buying the most expensive paints and brushes doesn't mean you can paint the *Mona Lisa*."

Mika giggled. "That's true!"

"Besides, a lot of photographers, and even filmmakers now, are using their phones instead of those big, fancy cameras," Jenny pointed out. "Have you seen Alisa's latest music video? One of the reasons everyone keeps talking about it is because the whole thing was shot on a phone!"

"Oh, right. I heard about that!" Mika said, thinking back. "And anyway, it's not like having a fancy camera and lens would have helped me find a theme for my assignment." Her stomach dropped a little at the thought.

"Have you gone through all of your photos from this week?" Jenny asked. "Maybe something will catch your eye!"

"I have, but all I see is New York City," Mika replied, pulling out her phone. "When we went to the escape room, I thought that maybe my theme could have something to do with food, but . . . I don't know. I don't think that's exactly what Mrs. Ibarra was looking for."

She handed her phone to Jenny, who opened the photos app. "'The Dress'?" she read out loud, pointing to one of the folders.

Mika nodded. "Oh, yeah—I saved the pictures I took of the dresses to a different folder so I could stay organized and find them quickly. It's just the shots of Samantha Foster and Alisa. See?"

As Jenny looked through the album, Mika was suddenly struck by an idea. "Can I try something really quickly?" she asked.

"Yeah, go for it," Jenny said, handing Mika back her phone. With her nose wrinkled in concentration, Mika tapped at her screen. As she was working, Andy wandered back to where they were standing and tried to look over Mika's shoulder to see what she was doing.

"Wait, let me finish first!" Mika mumbled.

"Okay, okay. Fine!" Andy laughed as he backed away.

The wait was worth it. When she had finished, Mika proudly held her phone out for Jenny and Andy to see. Watching Jenny swipe through the album had inspired her to use one of her photo-editing apps to create one image out of two photos. On the left was Samantha in her off-the-shoulder lavender dress, standing beneath the spotlight onstage. On the right was Alisa moving past the balcony doors in her cream-colored dress, like a ghost haunting the halls of Lincoln Center.

"Wow, nice job! It's so cool to see Mom's designs on her clients. The dresses look amazing!" Jenny marveled.

"They really do," Mika agreed. "I wonder if . . . Do you think Aunt Kei could use these photos in her presentation with the sketches?"

Jenny's face lit up. "Ooh, that's a great idea!" Then she grabbed Mika's arm excitedly. "Wait. Remember Brianna Richardson from dinner the other night? She was at the office this morning because she hired my mom to style her for her shoot today."

"That's a big deal. Maybe she'll be wearing something from Aunt Kei's new collection. We'll probably be able to see her at the game tonight," Andy said enthusiastically.

"Really?" Mika exclaimed. "If I can get a photo of her, I could make a triptych!" That was another term Mika had learned in photography club: three images side by side.

"Perfect," Jenny said, grinning. "Three of her famous clients in different New York City venues, all wearing her amazing designs. The buyers will *love* it."

Mika beamed, gazing down at her photos again. While this wouldn't make up for the loss of the origami dress, she hoped it would help Aunt Kei with her presentation tomorrow.

CHAPTER EIGHTEEN
ANDY

ONLY TEN MINUTES INTO their time at Madison Square Garden, Andy thought he might have taken almost as many videos on his phone as Mika had taken photos. After all, it was the "World's Most Famous Arena" for a reason. He texted at least ten of them to Devon, who simply responded with a photo of his television at home and the word SAME followed by a tongue-out emoji.

"Look at this, Mika!" Andy said, grinning as he showed her his phone. "Devon's getting ready to watch the game in his living room right now. I bet he wishes he was here with us!"

Mika laughed. "Maybe he'll see us! We should stand up and wave!" she joked as she jumped to her feet and started waving in every direction.

"We should've made signs for Lily and Po," Andy added, and his sister laughed.

The Kudos had arrived at the arena early to watch pregame warm-ups and were sitting in great seats at center court, halfway up the lower bowl. Andy could see the cameramen and -women down on the hardwood, but he doubted Devon would be able to spot him in this massive crowd, even if the cameras were pointed right in their direction.

Andy, Mika, and Dad all wore the USC shirts they'd packed just for this game. Andy was also wearing his favorite basketball sneakers, even though Mika had pointed out the obvious. He was there as a fan, not as a player. Since Mom was working, she was wearing a simple maroon dress that Aunt Kei had picked out for her. Andy could see her with a few journalists in the media seats on the other side of the court close to where Brianna Richardson's broadcast booth overlooked the game.

"So, that's one of Aunt Kei's dresses?" he asked Mika, pointing at Brianna.

She nodded eagerly. "Yeah! But I think it's actually pants, not a skirt," she added as Brianna stood up to organize her notes and have her mic adjusted by a crew member. Andy saw that Mika was right; what he had originally thought was a black dress was actually a jumpsuit.

"Oh, this is perfect!" Mika said, leaping to her feet. Andy watched as she framed Brianna on her screen. One of the other analysts got up to wave at the fans in a nearby section and did a silly dance. Brianna tilted her head back and laughed with the rest of the crowd as Mika took her shot.

"That's a good one!" Andy told her.

The USC band sat in a box on one end of the court, their instruments glinting in the light as they began to play the school's fight song. By the baskets, cheerleaders leaped up with their pom-poms in hand and began their routine while the crowd clapped along. The moment USC's fight song finished, Duke's band launched into its own, which made Andy and Mika laugh. Even the bands were competing tonight.

It looked like every seat in the arena was being filled, and many people were either wearing gold and cardinal red for USC, or white and royal blue for Duke. However, Andy spotted a few other familiar jerseys, including the blue and crimson of Kansas and the blue and gold of West Virginia, the two teams that had just been eliminated the other day.

"Why do you think those fans bought tickets for this game even after their own teams lost?" Mika asked Dad as two men in West Virginia shirts passed their row, heading up the stairs toward the concourse.

"Elite Eight game tickets are usually sold in packages," Dad explained. "A lot of fans whose teams are in the Sweet Sixteen travel to see the games and buy tickets hoping their teams advance."

"Dad's right," Andy said, nodding. "At the end of the

day, basketball fans love the sport and rep their teams no matter what. You've gotta believe—it's March Madness. I think USC is gonna win this game and go to the Final Four!"

Dad laughed. "That's a good attitude to have. You know that USC is actually the underdog in this game, right?"

"Nope," Andy said, grinning. "Not with Kian Jacobs, they aren't."

He pointed to the muscular USC point guard who was executing a variety of fun and complex handshakes with his teammates. Many of the game highlights Andy had watched over the last few months had been of Kian.

"He's averaging twenty points, six assists, and four and a half rebounds per game this season," Andy told Mika and Dad. "And Mom told me he's probably going to be one of the top picks in the NBA draft this year!"

"Trust me, I know Kian is talented," Dad said with a smile. "But Duke is a powerhouse with a great coach and they'll be tough to beat. Although being an underdog isn't necessarily a bad thing—especially during March Madness. Anything can happen in the tournament!"

The buzzer sounded, and Andy felt a jolt of excitement as the players moved from the benches to center court for the opening tip-off. The atmosphere was electric! Everyone in the arena was on their feet and cheering as the referee tossed the ball into the air and the players scrambled to gain possession. The game had begun! Andy, glasses on, barely blinked as he kept his eyes glued to the action that unfolded on the court. As much as Andy loved watching basketball highlights on YouTube and TV, it was different to actually be at the game *for real*—he could see and hear everything! The squeak of sneakers on the hardwood, the coaches shouting and pacing on the sidelines, and the chatter of the crowd that quickly rose to a roar when someone hit a shot.

And of course, the players themselves were astonishing. Somehow, in person, they seemed larger than life— and not just because most of them were so tall. Their strength, their speed, and their agility as they deftly dribbled and changed directions was a feat to behold. Kian Jacobs was particularly incredible. He seemed to know the exact location of every single player in the game, at all times. His passes were made with crisp precision—sometimes they almost seemed telepathic, as if he knew where his teammates would be before they were even there. Andy pointed this out to Mika and explained that this ability was called court vision.

"It's almost like how you seem to be able to capture photos at exactly the right moment!" Andy said. Mika blushed happily.

After a frenetic half of play, the scoreboard read DUKE 43, USC 40. Andy slouched back into his seat as the buzzer sounded. He was tired just from watching!

"What a game!" Dad said as he got up to stretch his legs. "That was so intense, I feel like this halftime break is for me—I'm thirsty! Want to get something to drink?"

"Frozen lemonade!" Mika said immediately, jumping up. "I saw the stand when we came in; I know where it is. I'll go with you! Want anything, Andy?"

"If the line isn't too long, can you please get me a hot dog or something? I'm starving!" Andy said as his stomach rumbled.

Andy stood and stretched as Dad and Mika passed him to head up the steps. The USC cheerleaders had taken the court while the band launched into their own performance on the sidelines, the deep *booms* of the bass drums echoing around the arena. He spotted Mom on the far side of the court, chatting with one of her colleagues. Brianna appeared on the jumbotron, seated at a desk with a host and another analyst, breaking down the first half of the game.

When the half-court shot contest began, Andy leaned forward and watched as a boy, not much older than him, jogged nervously to the center of the floor. It was announced on the overhead speaker that if he made the shot, the entire section that the Kudos were sitting in would receive vouchers for free personal pizzas. This really got Andy's attention. He knew he already had a hot dog coming his way, but before the game, Jenny had taken Mika and Andy to the Museum of Modern Art. It was a quick visit, and while he was glad they had gotten to see a New York City museum, he had worked up a big appetite with all of the brisk walking they had done around the city that day.

He stood and cheered with the crowd, willing the boy to make the miracle shot. Taking several steps back for a running start, he heaved the ball. Andy held his breath along with the rest of the arena as it soared in a perfect arc right toward the hoop—then clanged off the rim. So close! Everyone groaned, then cheered for the boy as he waved apologetically and jogged off the court.

Next up were the T-shirt cannons and the crowd went wild, waving their arms. Andy stood and waved frantically as one of the guys pointed the cannon in his direction. A rolled-up T-shirt flew at him, and Andy instinctively flung his arm out. It slapped right into his outstretched hand.

"Hey, nice catch!" cried the woman in the row in front of him.

Andy couldn't believe it. "Look, I caught a shirt!" he exclaimed, unfolding it to show Mika and Dad as they returned with spoons, napkins, three frozen lemonades, and Andy's hot dog.

"Wow!" Mika said.

"Is that for me?" Dad teased.

Andy laughed. "I'm going to give this one to Jenny.

Hopefully she'll need it next fall when she's a USC student!"

He rolled the shirt back up, then took his frozen lemonade and hot dog from Mika. After taking a few bites, Andy turned his attention to the jumbotron to watch the fan "dance cam" and a video montage of March Madness history.

Eventually, his gaze wandered back down to Brianna as she concluded her segment. She got up and walked over to join Mom, the flowy black pants of her jumpsuit billowing slightly as she moved. Andy remembered watching Samantha stride onstage in the lavender dress, and then catching a glimpse of Alisa twirling as she passed the balcony doors. Three similar, but not identical, designs.

Something was bothering him. He couldn't quite put his finger on it but kept his eyes on Brianna as he nudged Mika.

"Hey, can I see those pictures of Samantha and Alisa again?"

"Sure!" Mika balanced her frozen lemonade on her leg as she handed her phone over.

Andy devoured the rest of his hot dog as he studied the photos. He thought of the origami dress—one dress that could take on all three of these forms and more. The pattern Aunt Kei had showed them in her binder looked so complicated. Andy felt unsettled when he thought about how hard Aunt Kei must have worked on that design, and that dress. He wished he could have found it in time for her presentation.

If only he'd realized that the garment bags had been switched sooner! They would've been able to find the dress at Zoey's Thrift Shop before someone else had bought it. That was actually part of what was bothering Andy. The dress had arrived at the thrift shop on Monday. But yesterday, Zoey had still been unpacking the latest donations. It seemed odd to Andy that Aunt Kei's dress had not only been hung on the racks but had also been found *and* bought by Wednesday. Especially considering that it was damaged.

The buzzer sounded, and the crowd began to clap and cheer as the teams returned to the court. Andy quickly handed Mika's phone back and pushed all thoughts of the origami dress out of his mind as the game resumed.

While the first half had been intense, the second half was nothing short of astonishing. Both teams seemed to be pushing themselves harder than before. Even from this distance, Andy could see sweat running down their faces as they tore up and down the court. One moment, USC would pull ahead; a few seconds later, Duke would score again. The game was virtually tied throughout the fourth quarter. As the last minute ticked down on the scoreboard, it was clear that this would be a game to remember.

Andy yelled along with the crowd during the entirety of the final timeout. It was fun being as loud and rowdy as possible. Every person in the arena was on their feet and Dad had lifted Mika so she could see the court. The score was tied 88 to 88—USC had possession with only seven seconds left on the clock. Duke had used up all of their fouls and would have to play smart defense to send the game into overtime. Andy held his breath as the ball was inbounded from beyond half-court to Kian Jacobs. Immediately, Kian was surrounded by two Duke players as they attempted to trap him and steal the ball. He managed to protect the ball from his defenders and found a narrow window to whip a pass to the corner where a teammate stood waiting. A Duke forward appeared, seemingly out of nowhere, and the USC player no longer had an open shot. Pivoting, he was forced to pass the ball back to Kian, who had darted into the lane to get open. With only three and a half seconds left on the game clock, Kian snatched the ball out of the air, spun around, and took an off-balance shot. The ball left his hands with less than a second left and soared in a graceful arc over the outstretched fingertips of the other players, and then—

Swish! The ball fell through the hoop as the game clock hit zero and the final buzzer sounded.

"Wow! Clutch!" Dad yelled, pumping his fist in the air as the arena erupted into frenzied screams and cheers while the USC players swarmed Kian Jacobs in celebration. Andy whooped and hollered along with everyone else, laughing when the woman in the USC shirt who'd been sitting in front of Mika stood up on her seat and did a victory dance.

"That was insane! I can't believe it!" she cried, waving her arms wildly. Next to her, a girl who must have been her daughter took out her phone and giggled uncontrollably as she recorded her mother's celebration.

Over an hour later, when the Kudos finally arrived back at their hotel, Andy still felt wide-awake. They'd stopped at a halal cart to pick up some food, and Andy held the containers as Mika opened the door.

He only half listened as Mom and Dad continued to talk about the most exciting moments of the game, and what USC's chances were next week when they played Arizona. Andy found his mind wandering back to the origami dress pattern Aunt Kei showed them. Every time he pictured it, he felt as if he were almost on the verge of realizing something.

It wasn't until he woke up the next morning that it dawned on him.

Andy sat bolt upright in bed. "Mika!"

"Mmph." Mika's face was buried in her pillow. "Whu time issit?"

"Can I see your phone again?"

Without moving her head, Mika gestured to the night table between them, where her phone was charging. Andy grabbed it and opened the photos app, scrolling back until he reached the pictures Mika had taken the previous day in Professor Miller's classroom.

"Mika," he said, and this time his sister sat up groggily and peered at him.

"What's wrong?" she said, yawning. "Our alarm hasn't even gone off yet!"

Andy took a deep breath.

"I know who bought the origami dress."

CHAPTER NINETEEN
MIKA

MIKA RUBBED HER EYES, trying to fully wake up. She was pretty sure she'd misheard her brother. "Sorry, what?"

"I know who bought the dress from the thrift shop," Andy repeated. He was already throwing off his comforter and getting to his feet.

"How?" Mika said, frowning.

In response, Andy held out her phone. On the screen, Mika saw the photo she'd taken of the mannequin wearing what had looked like Aunt Kei's dress in Professor Miller's classroom.

"I don't get it." Mika pushed back her comforter and took her phone. "Are you saying Professor Miller has the original dress?"

"No!" Andy sounded excited. "Think about it. That dress is the only one that looks just like the origami dress. It's practically the same color, and it has the right neckline."

"But it's not the dress. The one on the mannequin wasn't even finished yet."

"Exactly!" Andy said. "One of Professor's Miller's students is making it for a personal project. And she said she's been struggling with it. Probably because it has a really complicated *pattern.*"

Mika remembered the pattern Aunt Kei had shown them at dinner. "Right—but nobody stole Aunt Kei's notes and the pattern."

Andy nodded. "But what if they saw a really cool dress at a thrift shop and then tried to figure out the pattern and recreate it?"

Mika's mouth fell open. "Oh! Wait . . . you think Professor Miller's student bought the dress?"

"It makes sense, doesn't it?" Andy pulled out his phone. "I'm going to text Jenny now. I don't remember the student's name, do you?"

"Umm . . ." Mika racked her brain as Andy typed. "Taylor something? Tiffany?"

Andy stared at his screen. A few seconds later, he grinned. "Jenny remembered . . . Tina Shah!"

"Yeah, that's it!"

"Jenny's asking why I want to know," Andy told Mika, thumbs flying as he responded to his cousin. The moment he hit send, Andy's smile faltered a little. He was starting to doubt himself.

"What's up?" Mika asked, looking at him curiously.

"I don't know," Andy said, sighing. "Maybe I've got it wrong. I mean, I've been wrong about every other theory I've had so far."

"So?" Mika pointed to the mystery novel on the night table between their beds. "Do the detectives in those books you read always solve the crime on their first try?"

"No," Andy admitted. "Still . . ." He stopped when his phone buzzed again. Glancing down, Andy saw another text from Jenny. He read it twice, and then a third time for good measure. "Mika, you aren't going to believe this . . ." Looking up, Andy grinned at his sister. "Jenny texted Noah to tell him my theory, and guess what Noah told her?"

"What?"

"Noah did some quick digging and found out that Tina Shah *works part-time at the thrift shop*!"

"*No. Way.*"

"Apparently, she helps repair and restore damaged items." Andy started to pace, thinking out loud as he did: "Remember when we went to the thrift shop? Zoey was still unpacking the donations from Monday—she told us she hadn't finished yet! I thought it was weird that Aunt Kei's dress had been unpacked *and* bought so fast . . . especially because it had a rip!"

"It needed repairs!" Mika jumped out of bed. "Maybe Tina found it and fixed the tear."

"And then she purchased it before Zoey could put it out on the racks!"

The Kudo kids beamed at one another.

"So if we can find Tina this morning . . ." Mika began.

Andy finished her thought: "We can get the dress back in time for Aunt Kei's presentation!"

Half an hour later, the Kudo kids headed down to the lobby to wait for Jenny. Mika and Andy had filled their parents in on everything, and now Mom and Dad were checking out at the reception desk.

"They're going to let us keep our luggage here until we have to leave for the airport," Dad said when he rejoined Mika and Andy.

"Glad we aren't going to be lugging our suitcases all over Manhattan!" Mika glanced out the window and spotted her cousin pushing through the revolving door. "There's Jenny!"

She and Andy raced to the door as Jenny walked into the lobby. "Did you ask Noah to call Tina?" Andy asked.

"Yeah, he tracked down her number and sent a bunch of texts too, but she hasn't responded," Jenny replied.

Mika frowned. "Really? That's kind of weird, isn't it?"

"Ugh! We have no idea where she is!" Andy said with a groan.

"I didn't say that," Jenny said, her head tilted. "You two aren't the only detectives in the family."

"What do you mean?" Mika asked.

Jenny wiggled her phone with a wry smile. "I found her on Instagram, and she just shared this on her story an hour ago."

She held her phone out, and Mika saw a photo of a group of young women seated around a table on a small patio. They were all dressed up—but one dress caught Mika's eye immediately.

"The origami dress!" she squealed, pointing to the woman with light brown skin and waist-length dark hair in a long ponytail. "Tina's wearing it under her jacket!"

"'Birthday brunch for my best friend in the world! #besties #BrunchBunch,'" Andy read from the caption. "This says they're at Helena's Café on the Upper West Side. Is that close?"

"It's maybe fifteen or twenty minutes on the train," Jenny said as Mom and Dad joined them. "Are you sure you guys want to do this? It's your last morning in New York City! I can go by myself."

"Of course we do!" Mom exclaimed. "Anything to help Kei with her presentation. Does she know you kids figured out who has the dress?"

"Not yet," Jenny said. "She left for the office super early this morning to get everything ready."

Together, the group left the hotel and headed to the subway station down the street. While Mika sat next to Andy on the train, Jenny, Mom, and Dad discussed how they were going to get to Aunt Kei's office if they managed to find Tina.

"Even if Tina does agree to let us have the dress back," Mika said in a low voice, "it's not like she can just give it to us at the restaurant. She'll have to go home and change first."

Andy nodded, looking nervous. "And we don't know where she lives. This could take a while and we don't have all day."

"Aunt Kei's presentation is at eleven." Mika glanced at the time on her phone. "It's already past ten!"

Jenny must have been watching the clock too, because when the train finally reached their stop, she practically bolted out onto the platform. The Kudos raced after her, weaving through the crowd and past a trio of musicians playing for a group of onlookers. Once they were up on the street, Jenny led the way through the intersection and turned right onto Amsterdam.

"There!" she exclaimed, pointing. Up ahead, Mika saw a white awning with the words HELENA'S CAFÉ in fancy script. The outdoor seating area was small, but to their collective relief, they spotted a group of women at one of the tables that Mika recognized from Tina's Instagram story. Their dishes had been cleared, and

Tina was taking the bill from the waiter when Jenny and the Kudos reached them.

"You're Tina, right?!" Jenny said, gasping for breath. All of the women looked up in surprise and Tina looked especially confused.

"Yes? Do I know you?"

"Not exactly," Jenny replied, fanning her face as she spoke. "I'm friends with Noah Wilson."

"Oh! Yeah, I know Noah." Tina smiled a little, though her brows were still arched. "Um . . . What's up?"

Jenny swallowed, glancing back at the Kudos. It dawned on Mika how ridiculous this story was probably going to sound to Tina—or worse, she might even think they were accusing her of stealing! Mika pictured the mannequin in Professor Miller's classroom with the partially constructed dress Tina had been working on, and inspiration struck.

"I can explain. The dress you're wearing," Mika said, stepping forward. "It was designed by my aunt—her mom," she added, nodding to Jenny. "Kei Taguchi. She's a—"

Tina's face lit up. "What! Really?" she exclaimed as she got to her feet. "Of course I know who Kei Taguchi is. I *love* her work. Kei is a celeb stylist, you guys," she told her friends, who looked impressed. "I didn't know she also had her own line of clothing. I found this in the donation pile at work on Monday . . . It had a tear, and after I repaired it, I decided I had to have it. That's so weird!"

She smoothed down the front of the dress as she spoke, and Jenny gave Mika a grateful look. "Actually, it gets weirder," Jenny said hurriedly as she told Tina and her friends more about the mystery of the missing dress. They listened with rapt attention, and by the time Jenny finished, Tina was giggling.

"Oh my gosh, I can't believe you thought Professor Miller *stole* it," she said, covering her mouth with her hand. "That's too funny."

"The thing is, our aunt Kei's presentation is in . . ." Andy paused to glance at his phone. "Half an hour! And we really want her to be able to show the buyers this dress in person."

"I know you bought it fair and square," Jenny added. "But could we maybe borrow it, just for a few hours?"

Tina was already picking up her purse. "Are you kidding? I'd love to meet Kei Taguchi!"

"You mean you'll come with us?" Mika cried, clapping her hands in excitement.

Tina beamed. "Of course! You said you're short on time, right? Lead the way!"

Her friends waved as she said rushed goodbyes and hurried around the patio gate. Mika felt a surge of hope and excitement as the six of them headed back to the subway station. They had found the dress and still had a chance to help Aunt Kei! She hung back with her mom as the group ran down the stairs, opening the camera app on her phone and snapping a few shots of Tina swiping her MetroCard at the turnstile.

This train was fortunately less crowded than the one they'd taken earlier, and they clung to the poles and talked as it raced from stop to stop. Tina gripped the pole closest to the doors, the skirt of her dress swishing around her legs as the train rumbled down the tracks.

Mika couldn't resist. "Can I take your picture?"

Tina did a little pose, swinging her long ponytail over her shoulder. "Of course!"

She struck another pose, one elbow wrapped around the pole while her free hand pointed up at the ceiling. Jenny plus Andy and Mika's parents laughed as she took the shot.

"How about one of you sitting down?" Mika asked, pointing to a newly vacated seat. Tina hurried over and sat, crossing her legs and tilting her head. Mika snapped the photo just as the doors slid open.

"Ooh, let's get one of you pretending to walk into the train!" Mika exclaimed, and Tina hurried over to the doors. Most of the other passengers were watching and smiling as Tina quickly stepped out and in again, raising both arms and doing a little spin.

Perfect, Mika thought, smiling to herself as she imagined how this picture would look next to the ones she took of Samantha, Alisa, and Brianna.

"We're getting out at the next stop. Be ready!" Dad said. Mika gazed out at the platform, watching as people moved up and down the stairs. A woman playing steel drums laughed as two little kids began to dance a few feet away from her, hopping up and down to the beat.

Mika was so amused by their energy and dancing that it was almost a full minute before she realized something was wrong.

"Why aren't the doors closing?" she wondered out loud.

Jenny chewed her lip. "I don't know. Maybe—"

"*Attention, ladies and gentlemen, due to a faulty signal light at the next stop, this train will be terminating here. Transfer is available to the B, D, F, and M trains . . .*"

As the conductor continued, Mika looked from her parents to Jenny. "What should we do? Can we take another train?"

Jenny shook her head. "Not to that stop."

"How far are we from Kei's office?" Mom asked, consulting the subway map hanging near the door.

"Close-ish. Four or five blocks, I think."

"What are we waiting for? We can still make it." Tina was already heading for the door. "New York City is a walking city! And besides, I'm always up for a morning jog!"

Laughing, the Kudos and Jenny followed her onto the platform. Mika and Andy raced up the stairs, Jenny and

Tina in front of them, their parents right on their heels.

"I'm so glad we don't have our suitcases," Mika said, gasping for breath as they finally reached the street.

Andy laughed. "No kidding. That would be rough!"

The four blocks to Aunt Kei's office felt extra-long. By the time they reached the white stone building, Mika thought this was an even better workout than when the Kudos had raced through LAX to make their flight to Tokyo. She pulled off her jacket as they entered the building and checked in at the security desk. Once they had all been handed VISITOR stickers, they crammed onto the elevator, laughing as Andy made an exaggerated wheezing sound in the corner.

"Phew!" he said as he wiped sweat from his forehead. "I'm glad this building has air conditioning. What time is it? Did we make it?"

"We're here with one minute to go!" Jenny said triumphantly as the doors slid open. "Her conference room is right down this way."

She led the group past a few models wearing Aunt Kei's designs to a set of double doors at the end of the hall, which she pushed open—and then froze.

"Oh! Sorry, Mom, I didn't know you'd already started!"

Mika skidded to a halt behind her, her eyes widening at the sight of Aunt Kei standing at the head of a long table. Four people sat on one side, while three sat on the other, and every head was turned in their direction.

"Jenny? Karen?" Aunt Kei looked perplexed, and slightly worried. "Is everything okay?"

"Yes! We're so sorry to barge in like this, Kei," Mom said, stepping inside. "But, well . . . we thought this might help with your presentation."

Mika and Andy moved farther into the room to let Tina in. Aunt Kei's face lit up when she saw the origami dress.

"*You found it!*" she cried, gesturing for Tina to join her at the head of the table. "Well, this is a *huge* surprise. Thank you all so much!"

"Of course!" Jenny looked profoundly relieved. "We'll just step out so you can get back to your presentation."

"No, no, stay!" Aunt Kei smiled around at the buyers seated at the table. "None of you will mind if my family watches, will you? We've had quite the week—you won't believe it when I tell you what a journey this dress has been on! And I'm not sure how they did it, but it wouldn't have made it here without my amazing family."

"I can't wait to hear it!" said the man seated closest to Aunt Kei.

"That dress is stunning," added the red-haired woman next to him. Tina beamed and did a little twirl.

"This dress is actually the centerpiece of my collection," Aunt Kei said, and Mika saw that each buyer had a large portfolio laid out in front of them. Even from the back of the room, she recognized the sketches of Aunt Kei's dresses. "There was a little mishap on Monday and . . . I believe the dress was torn, but I'm glad you can see it in person today."

Tina nodded, gesturing to the waistline. "There was a little tear here, but I repaired it. I'm Tina, by the way. I'm a student at FIT," she added.

"Is that so?" Aunt Kei peered closely at the waistline of the dress. "Goodness . . . I have to say, I can't even see your stitching. You're quite the seamstress!"

Tina looked ready to burst with happiness. "Oh my gosh, you have no idea how much that means to me! I *love* your work—and the design for this dress is mind-blowingly complex and creative!"

The buyers laughed. "Well, what are you waiting for, Kei?" the red-haired woman said with a grin. "Let's see your collection."

Aunt Kei beamed. "Originally I intended to save the best for last, but hey—why not start off with a bang instead?"

Mika stood between Jenny and Andy as Aunt Kei launched into an explanation of the sustainable, convertible design of the dress. As she spoke, Tina listened intently, holding her arms out when Aunt Kei began to rearrange the sections of fabric. Mika watched in amazement as she demonstrated how the dress worked, revealing hidden clips and a small zipper that allowed sections of the fabric to move, changing first the sleeves, then the neckline, then the waistline.

"And that's just what you can do while wearing the dress," Aunt Kei added. "There are even more options if you alter it before putting it on. For example . . ."

As Aunt Kei flipped her copy of her portfolio to a new page, Mika leaned closer to Jenny. "Tina turned out to be a great model!" she whispered. "*And* a great seamstress!"

Jenny nodded, her eyes shining with pride as she watched her mom. "You know, Mom mentioned that she might want to hire an intern this summer. I bet Tina would be interested!"

Mika had to agree. Tina was listening intently to every word Aunt Kei said, even standing on tiptoe so she could see the portfolio spread open on the table.

"Ooh!" Mika exclaimed with delight. Andy glanced at her, concerned.

"Are you okay?"

Mika nodded fervently, bouncing on the balls of her feet. Her face had split into a smile that showed all of her teeth. "I think I finally have a theme for my photography assignment!"

CHAPTER TWENTY

ANDY

"DOUBLE PEPPERONI WITH GARLIC KNOTS!"

Andy leaned back as Dad set the extra-large pizza and basket of garlic knots down. The Kudos, Aunt Kei, and Jenny had decided to squeeze in a celebratory lunch after Aunt Kei's presentation. And as Dad had pointed out, they couldn't leave the city without experiencing a slice of real New York–style pizza!

"All seven buyers are on board!" Jenny said as she grabbed a slice. "I still can't believe it, Mom. I mean, I *can*, because your whole line is amazing, but . . ."

Aunt Kei laughed, her eyes dancing. "Thanks, hon. I'm so grateful to you—to all three of you!" she added, raising her bottled iced tea in a toast to Mika and Andy. "The demonstration with the origami dress was what clinched the deal. The buyers loved it!"

"That girl Tina looked almost as excited as you, Kei," Mom said with a grin. "Weren't you mentioning that you were looking to hire an intern? I think she'd be fabulous."

"Oh, I had a little chat with her after the presentation and we exchanged contact info—she'll be *perfect*," Aunt Kei replied before taking a bite out of a warm garlic knot.

Andy sprinkled oregano and red pepper flakes on his pizza, and then attempted to pick it up. The slice was so enormous that he had a hard time holding it up without it drooping.

"Hang on, Andy!" Dad said with a laugh after observing Andy's struggles. "There's a special technique to eating New York–style pizza. Let me show you." Andy watched as Dad folded his slice in half, almost like a sandwich, then took a gigantic bite. Laughing, Andy did the same thing. The sauce was sweet and a little bit spicy, the cheese warm and gooey, and the crust was chewy but had the perfect amount of crispiness.

"Yummm!! It's *so* good!!" Mika exclaimed before taking another bite. Andy nodded enthusiastically in agreement since his mouth was too full to talk.

"Mika, did I hear you say that you figured out a theme for your photography assignment?" Jenny asked.

Mika's face glowed. "I think so! Hold on, let me show you . . ."

Andy grabbed a garlic knot, watching as his sister pulled out her phone. She tapped the screen, then held it up so everyone could see it. He quickly recognized the photo of Samantha Foster onstage in the lavender dress.

"I've decided that my theme will be a collection of these five photos," Mika said. As she spoke, she swiped through the other images: Alisa running through the hall in the cream-colored dress, the mannequin wearing the unfinished dress, Brianna at the game in the black jumpsuit, and Tina posing in front of the open train doors on the subway. "Each photo was captured in an iconic New York City location—a Broadway theatre, Lincoln Center, FIT, Madison Square Garden, and the subway. I'm going to call it 'Dressing Up New York'!"

"Mika, that's such a good idea!" Mom exclaimed.

"I *love* it!" Jenny added.

"They're all going to look so cool side by side," Andy said, grinning at his sister. "Are you going to get them printed?"

"Yeah!" Mika looked pleased. "Mrs. Ibarra even said some of the assignments might get displayed in one of the cases by the front of the school."

"That's great! While we're speaking about exciting breakthroughs," Jenny said, turning to Andy, "I thought you'd like to know that your amazing detective work this week has inspired me."

Andy paused, another bite of pizza already in his mouth. "Really?"

Jenny nodded, her eyes sparkling in a way that made her look even more like Aunt Kei than usual. "I finally got an idea for my first screenplay—I think it's going to be a mystery!"

Andy finished chewing and swallowed before reacting to his cousin's announcement. "Seriously? That's so cool!"

"And since you're such an avid reader and solver of mysteries, maybe when I finish the first draft, you can read it and give me a little feedback?" Jenny asked. "I know you're busy with your photography club, but you can read it too, Mika!"

"I *definitely* want to read it!" Mika nodded.

"Same!" Andy said. "Although now that you mention being busy . . . I think I have a new project, too."

All eyes turned toward him. "You do?" Mika asked in surprise. "What is it?"

Andy paused. What if his family thought this was a silly idea? Then he shook off the thought and cleared his throat, looking at Mika.

"Seeing how much you've loved photography club this year got me thinking," he said slowly. "I want a creative hobby like that, too. I mean, beta testing for the Masked Medalist was great, and I learned a lot about different types of games, but I had this idea. I texted Tyler and Devon last night to see what they thought, and, well . . ." Andy took a deep breath. "We're going to try designing our own game. An escape room app!"

"What?!" Mika was beaming. "That's *so awesome*!"

"I think that's a terrific idea, Andy!" Dad said as Mom, Aunt Kei, and Jenny nodded in agreement.

"Thanks," Andy said, pleased. "I looked on our local library's website last night and they actually have a coding club for middle school students that meets every Saturday at ten. Would it be okay if I joined?"

"Of course!" Mom grinned at Andy. "I can drive you. This is a *great* project. I can't wait to see what you guys develop. Maybe I'll even play the game myself!"

Aunt Kei chuckled. "Get your mom to be your beta tester, Andy. If you can design a game that even *she* can play, you'll be the most successful game developer on the planet."

Andy laughed along with everyone else, picking up a garlic knot. As he tried to cram the entire thing into his mouth, Mika leaned over and nudged his side with her elbow.

"It's funny," she said. "Our vacation is pretty much over, but I don't feel as sad as I usually do at the end of a trip."

"Smmm hrrrr," Andy mumbled as he attempted to finish chewing. He swallowed and nodded vigorously. "I'm definitely going to miss New York. And Aunt Kei and Jenny . . ."

"But we'll see them when they visit LA this summer," Mika pointed out. "And we'll see Jenny a whole lot more if she ends up coming out for college. And who knows where our next trip will be?!"

Andy smiled and felt content. Mika was right. He could happily explore New York City for another week. But at the same time, he was also looking forward to returning to school and seeing their friends. Plus, summer vacation wasn't too far away, and in the fall, Andy would be in the eighth grade. He was excited for what the future might hold for him and his sister. There was always another adventure to look forward to.

ACKNOWLEDGMENTS

Thank you for spending time with us and joining the Kudo Kids on this adventure! The response to our series from readers and supporters around the world has been incredible. We have felt energized and inspired by your warmth, kind comments, and pictures following the release of Book 1.

In our experience, meaningful projects are the result of passion, hard work, and most importantly, collaboration. We feel so much gratitude toward the remarkable group of people who helped bring this story to life.

Julie Rosenberg, thank you for believing in us. We feel very lucky that you always have the patience and energy to discuss every detail—even down to individual words. Your positivity brings out the best in us. You are an incredible editor, guide, and friend.

Michelle Schusterman, continuing to work with you has been wonderful. Exploring one of our favorite cities and crafting another mystery together has been really fulfilling—you are an amazing partner. Thank you for caring about Mika and Andy, humor, adventure, and food as much as we do.

Yaoyao Ma Van As, your illustrations are magical. You've brought our characters and scenes to life in such a beautiful way. Thank you for sharing your immense talent with us and our readers. Looking at this cover always makes us smile.

Elyse Marshall, connecting with you and working on any project always makes our day better. We appreciate your thoughtfulness so much. Thank you for taking such good care of us.

To the rest of our publishing team—Casey McIntyre, Alex Sanchez, Jen Klonsky, Gretchen Durning, Maria Fazio, Lindsey Andrews, Marinda Valenti, Jayne Ziemba, Lauren Festa, Christina Colangelo, Emily Romero, Alex Gerber, and Anna Elling—we are grateful for your continued support. Thank you for your collective efforts, creativity, and enthusiasm. We love this series and are very proud to be part of the Razorbill family.

Albert Lee and Mary Pender, Kudo Kids wouldn't have been possible without both of you. Telling stories is our passion—joining the literary world has enriched our lives and given us additional purpose and joy. Thank you for helping us continue to dream, create, and share.

Theresa Peters, Ty Flynn, and Jonathan Beckerman, thank you for being our amazing team.

Eva Chen, Virginia Nam, Justin Antony, Jackson Williams, Lauren Schutte, Ashley Yuki, Brown Bartholomew, Jeanne Yang, Edward Barsamian, Tina Lundgren, Alissandra Aronow, Kathy Bird, and Patrick Lee, thank you for your encouragement and friendship.

To our Book 1 blurbers, Kristi Yamaguchi, Elizabeth Eulberg, Bobby Hundreds, Lyla Lee, Scott Hamilton, Lindsey Vonn, Stephanie Garber, and Debbi Michiko Florence, thank you for your time, words, and early enthusiasm.

Greg Pak, Sarah Kuhn, and Preeti Chhibber, thank you for warmly welcoming us into the writing community on Twitter.

Thank you Bing Chen, Jeremy Tran, and the rest of Gold House for the work you do to create, foster, and support community. To our friends at Asia Society, U.S. Japan Council, and Japan America Society, thank you for welcoming us and championing this series.

Finally, Mom and Dad—your unconditional support and belief mean everything to us. We love you!

—Maia and Alex